WHISPERING OF ECHOES

A BECKER GRAY SHORT STORY BY

CHRIS WENDEL

Holden Publishing, Inc.

Holden Publishing, Inc.
5304 S Florida Ave, Ste 404
Lakeland, FL 33813

BOOKS BY CHRIS WENDEL

BECKER GRAY SERIES

Human After All

Whispering of Echoes

BUSINESS

Converting Customers to Clients: A Guide to Strengthening Your Business Relationships

On Strengthening Business Relationships

POETRY

Unfinished

This is for

    Holden

    Blake

    Taylor

    Kinsy

    Jonathan

    and

    Connor

CHAPTER 1

"Do you cut yourself?"

"Not physically."

Becker Gray stared at the ashtray on Frances Vandenhill's office desk. It looked like a pile of marbles melted into a drooping bowl-like structure. He wondered where it had come from. Did she have a child who made it for her at summer camp? And why an ashtray? Not many people smoked anymore. Did she?

Gray realized then that he knew nothing about his department-appointed therapist. He'd been seeing her for almost five months straight, and he couldn't think of anything specific he knew about her. In a city like Lakeland, Florida, Gray should know two out of five people just from living there his whole life. Add on his law enforcement background and community involvement, and he surmised he should, at least, know of three or four out of five people. So he thought it was odd that he didn't know of Frances Vandenhill before therapy.

"Then how?" she asked.

Gray didn't respond. Instead, he waited her out. Eventually she'd make a note on her pad of paper, realizing he was done talking, and move on. While ignoring her question, he scolded himself for not paying attention. He hated these sessions, even though he initiated them this stretch of time. He tried to keep the conversation at surface level, but every now and then she'd catch him not paying attention and he'd answer honestly. And then he'd find himself in a conversation he didn't want to have, like this one.

She didn't write in her pad though.

"Becker, have you made any new friends?"

"Where did that come from?"

Gray shifted in his seat, almost leaning away from her and her questions. It was the first time during this session that he'd adjusted his sitting position. Vandenhill made a note of that on her pad.

"I've been thinking about it lately for you." She leaned forward, countering his retreat. "You seem to enjoy your friendship with your partner, but I was thinking maybe you should meet someone who isn't connected to your work life."

"Why would I do that?"

Vandenhill smiled, happy – and surprised – that Gray was entertaining the idea. She responded, "Friendship enhances the human experience."

"I don't think so."

"You don't think friendships make peoples' lives better?"

"Not that," Gray said, moving in his seat again, narrowly closing his posture. "I don't think I'll be making any new friends."

Vandenhill noted his response, then asked, "Why?"

"I'm good." He dismissed the notion.

"The holidays are coming up. Friends are very important this time of year."

"Is that why you asked if I was a cutter? You think I'll kill myself this holiday season?"

"Since you brought it up ... "

Gray chuckled at her and the silly theory, but when she didn't move on to a new topic, he asked, "You're serious?"

She clicked her pen twice. It marked the end of a conversation, when she wanted to change the topic. "What are you doing for the holidays?"

"Nothing. On duty, I suppose."

"You won't see your parents? Or your brother?"

"My schedule doesn't really allow for that." Gray thought these questions were ridiculous. What did it matter if he saw his parents? Why did she care anyway?

"What about Detective Parker?" She slid her hips to the back of her chair again.

"I don't know what his plans are."

"I mean, will you spend time with him?"

Gray shrugged his shoulders. Then he remembered something, and he hoped sharing it would get her off his back. Within a few more questions. *There are always more questions.* "The mayor invited me to a Christmas party."

"The mayor?"

"I'm a big deal since the Pen Pal case." A smirk slid across his face, faux bragging. Right before he kicked off these sessions again with Vandenhill, he solved a case that thrust him into the national spotlight.

She laughed – he had a smart wit, when he let his guard down – but she didn't want to encourage that behavior. It was hard enough to get him talking. "Well, are you going to attend?"

"Sure."

It was a noncommittal response.

"I think you should."

Gray nodded, accepting her statement simply as information.

Wanting to use the rare moment of flowing communication with Gray, she moved on to the next subject, clicking her pen. "Have you picked out a vacation spot yet?"

"You've covered a lot of ground here, doc." He scooted to the front of the chair cushion, like he was positioning himself to stand and leave.

"How's that?" Vandenhill smiled, knowing the answer, and twirled the pen between her fingers.

"You've gone from me cutting myself to my family and now to my vacation. The cutting thing was new, but the rest we talk about all the time."

She tapped the pen against her pad. "The friendship topic was new too."

"I guess it was."

They both knew he was delaying the response. He waited for her to move on, and she waited for him to answer.

Finally, "Well?"

"Well what?" he asked.

His wit had lost whatever amusement it possessed earlier in the conversation.

"No." Agitation clearly in his tone. "I haven't done any of the homework you assigned." He stood to leave.

She stood too, clicking her pen. "Think more about it. I don't want to make it mandatory."

CHAPTER 2

Nicole Abernathy laced up her new sneakers, adorned with a colorful mix of purples, greys, reds, and yellows. They arrived via UPS before she came home from work. She had nearly run completely through the soles of her old athletic shoes, not having been able to afford a replacement pair. Two months ago, though, Nicole had accepted a promotion, and the raise that came with it afforded her two splurges: these new sneakers and a better brand of makeup.

She checked herself in the full-length mirror in her apartment bedroom – her face wiped clean of makeup, new shoes making her outfit look ragged, and her body not nearly where she wanted it. Yet she was as content as she'd ever been. Things were going in a good direction for her. Her reflection smiled back at her.

Nicole slipped her driver license in the hidden pocket of her running shorts and strapped on her advanced fitness tracker. Then she headed out the door.

It took Nicole 35 minutes to get from her apartment to the Fort Fraser Trail because of the heavy rush hour traffic. She parked Old Thunder, the name she had given her car the first time the muffler fell off, and tucked her set of keys into the same hidden pocket as her driver license. She stretched her hamstrings, quadriceps, and calves before running down the trail in her ongoing effort to improve her shape.

After only ten minutes sweat had spread across her body, making her ragged outfit adhere to her like skin. The new shoes bounced off the ground, propelling her forward, as if springs were attached to the bottom of her feet. And with every stride of her legs, more of her day's stress waned – the hectic pace of her new job; the feeling of uncertainty that she could fulfill the position's role; the fact that now she was the supervisor of the man she'd been pining over; the idea that she was pining over a man in the first place; and that she had used the word *pining*. She remembered how she looked in her mirror, and she decided she shouldn't be pining, obsessing, yearning, or whatever over any man. No, men should be dropping at her feet. She laughed to herself at the concept. That's not how her life had been. She was pretty, personable, fashionable, and available, but she just never had any real luck with men. She thought dating in her late 20s would be easy. *Not so much though,* she thought.

Soon all those thoughts were gone. Her mind fell blank. Literally nothing going on. Nicole became one with her body, measuring her breathing, her pace, and her heart rate – all by instinct. This was the reason she ran. To reach this point, to turn the world off. To push the bullshit away. To escape into a place and time where nothing existed. She never knew how long the feeling would last, but it didn't matter. Ten minutes. An hour. Who cared? As long as she escaped reality, this is what kept her alive, what kept her pure, what kept her focused.

Yes. Focus.

That was her every day: focus, drive, goals, betterment, dreams, and hopes.

It bred a persona of superiority. Not in a negative sense though. She never felt herself superior to other people. Maybe, she thought, she felt superior over the situation. She wasn't sure how to explain it. She just knew where she was in life at this moment wouldn't be where she'd be forever.

This was why running appealed to her so much. Eventually her current situation would wilt in her mind, leaving her with the ability to focus what was most important to her: goals.

Yes, goals.

The more people Nicole dealt with in the world, the more she became convinced that most people had no hopes, dreams, or goals. Most seemed content to let life pass them by. She couldn't understand it. The idea of waking up every morning simply to go to work before coming home every night to watch television and go to bed made her sick to her stomach. She remembered her parents coming home from work and sitting on the front porch, swaying back and forth in their rocking chairs. Every day. Her parents were awesome, wonderful people. There just was no way in hell could she imagine that lifestyle.

No, she wanted amazing things for herself. Her current job was only part of her plan. She was earning real world experience. She was finally making decent money. She had a good schedule – four days on, three off – which left her plenty of time to pursue her dreams of being a travel blogger.

Nicole, when she was 25 years old, met a wealthy man who had swept her off her feet. He was older and was nothing like the men her age. He was polite, spoke about important topics, treated her well, didn't wear his hat backwards, didn't get drunk on lite beer, and he wasn't close-minded. He was just like her. At least, in one way: he had drive and focus, and goals mattered. That was their initial connection. She loved that about him.

During their relationship, he took Nicole on his business trips. Once a month, they'd fly off together, and she'd experience wonders she never knew about. It was during those trips that she fell in love with travel. She wanted to spend her whole life flying around the world. What better way to do it than to make it a business?

The love of travel lasted longer than the relationship. After a year, she'd found out that three other women in their early twenties traveled with him too: each on a four-week rotation. So the guy had to go, and with him went those trips. Left behind was the desire to travel.

When she finally developed her business plan, she began traveling on her own dime. She'd spent two years building content for her blog launch, which was occurring in six weeks. At first, she focused on weekend trips around Florida. All the beaches had countless locations to feature. She then began driving up to eastern Georgia, featuring places like Jekyll Island and St. Simons. She made it as far north as Savannah, Tybee Island, and Hilton Head. More recently, she began looking at the last-minute trips airlines offered at a very low cost. She had a bag packed and ready to go, so every Friday night she'd find a deal and off she went – to Atlanta, New Orleans, Las Vegas, and Nashville. Wherever the best deal sent her.

During that time, Nicole had noticed that she seemed to have lost friends. The more she focused on this launch and traveling, the less time she had for friends. Now she only had a few people she saw outside of work, and she only rarely saw them. Reconnecting with friends was high on her to-do list, but it never seemed to happen. The launch was taking up so much of her time, money, and energy. She had to accept that to reach her goals. And she did. *Mostly.*

This promotion, though, should help. Instead of working five to seven days a week at two jobs, she could work one job four days a week and make more money than the two jobs she was working previously. That left time, she thought, to focus on her blog and business, as well as allow time to meet up with old friends.

Nicole realized her thoughts had sped up and her pace had slowed during her run. This was the opposite of what usually happened. She wanted more escape. She pumped her legs faster, hoping to find that place again where her mind shut off. She saw the dimming autumn sky ahead of her and noted the time on her fitness tracker, along with her heart rate and length of run – 5:43 p.m. The sun wouldn't set for almost 30 more minutes. She wondered if she should turn around and head back to her car, finishing the run on the path in the dark? Or, she figured the other option was to run another couple of miles to the city bus stop and catch one back to her car? Then it happened.

Her vision flipped. What was up was now down and vice versa, like she was watching it on a television or movie screen. Her brain saw it as if she were upright, which is where the confusion came in. It wasn't until Nicole's body slammed against the trail's hard, compacted dirt ground that her brain registered what had happened. She'd lost her balance and had fallen – tripped maybe – which was what she was afraid of by turning and running back to her car in the dark. The ground attacked her torso, arms and legs. With the next roll, her head connected with the ground. Everything went black.

Then she was dragged into the wooded area along the path.

CHAPTER 3

Awkward wasn't the right word to describe Gray at the mayor's holiday party. Confused was more like it. As in, why'd he attend? Parker was his only friend, and he wasn't there. He didn't appreciate small talk, but that's the only talk that seemed to come his way. He didn't like dressing up, but he'd bought a new shirt and pulled a tie he'd never worn from the depths of his closet. *What the hell am I doing?*

The mayor's two-story red-brick house was modestly furnished and decorated in earth tones. A lot of beige in the house. Despite the lack of color and the house having been built in the 1950s, the home seemed modern and contemporary. The floor plan was too open for a house built then. Gray figured that walls had been removed to create the inviting environment.

He sipped a fruit punch – he'd made sure it wasn't spiked. He stood before the table of hors d'oeuvres and wondered what to eat. He liked meats and cheeses, potatoes, and even vegetables, but not much of that was spread before him. Not the way he liked it served anyway. He saw tartare, hummus, pâté, some sort of olive based mush, and he thought he saw a tofu dish, which really made him question the food options and, yet again, why he was even there.

Wondering further, he grew curious about the hosts, Douglas and Morgan Beringer. Douglas had been a police officer for a handful of years. Gray had known him superficially a long time ago when they both were patrolmen. Douglas had been a bright star and had a promising career in the department. That was what everyone thought, Gray recalled, but the man left it behind when he graduated law school. He went on to build a successful practice with two partners before that firm broke apart. Douglas opened his own practice. He was successful then too. He hung that up – to a degree – and was voted in as mayor. Gray liked that Douglas had returned to his roots of serving the community. What he did recall about Douglas from their time together on the police force was that he wasn't a tartare and pâté kind of guy. Must've been the wife's thing.

As for the wife, Gray knew only who Morgan Beringer was from the media coverage of the election.

The Christmas tree caught his attention, and Gray decided to move closer to it. The decorated fir was more interesting to him than the people at the party. As an added bonus, if anyone decided to try to speak to him, he could bore them with a conversation about the tree.

The limbs were thick with bristles, and they must've been quite strong to hold all the ornaments. The tree was cluttered, but it still looked tasteful, artful even. Decorated in golds and red, the accessories included beaded garland, bulbs, orbs, tinsel, and a variety of unusually shaped hanging trinkets. Gray realized that the decorations matched those around the house – over the fireplace, strung across doorways, and the dining table centerpiece.

"Are you going to steal the tree?"

Gray startled slightly, turning to find the source of the voice.

"Mrs. Beringer." He greeted the mayor's wife. "No, I'm not. Do I look like I'm casing the place?"

Her tone was jovial and light. He tried to match it, which confused him further. Jovial and light weren't a component of his typical demeanor. He noticed that her red dress and the tone of her lightly browned skin matched the house decorations.

"You look uncomfortable."

"It's that obvious? I thought I was doing a good job of hiding it."

"You're not."

Morgan reached toward him, which resulted in Gray's tensing. She hesitated before continuing the extension of her arm and then she peeled a clear sticker off Gray's new shirt. She crumpled the sticker displaying the shirt size.

"New shirt," Gray mumbled, embarrassed. He wasn't embarrassed though that he left the sticker on the shirt. He was embarrassed that he'd purchased a new shirt for the evening. That showed he was looking forward to the night, which wasn't much within his normal behavior either.

"Have you tried the brioche lobster rolls?" Morgan asked.

"No." He didn't want to tell her he hadn't tried anything.

"I did." She shook her head. "I wouldn't, if I were you?"

"That bad?"

"Worse." She smiled, and warmth radiated toward Gray. "This isn't my kind of food. I'd much prefer Taco Tuesday at a sports bar than this."

Her statement seemed genuine, but Gray couldn't help thinking he was being played by a politician's wife.

"I find that hard to believe, Mrs. Beringer."

She laughed then leaned toward him. Her perfume and minty breath hugged him. She whispered when she spoke. "Don't tell any of Douglas' constituents, but it's true." She pushed her hand out in greeting. "It's Morgan, by the way. And I know who you are."

"And you still came to say hello?" He shook her hand – strong but soft to touch.

"Why wouldn't I? You're the hero police officer who caught the Pen Pal."

Gray wanted to roll his eyes at the statement but didn't. Instead, he said, "Don't tell Douglas' constituents, but he kind of caught himself."

She patted him on the shoulder.

"I doubt that, Becker."

Morgan's fingers nearly glided their way down Gray's arm, finishing the gesture by gripping Gray's hand. "I need to go speak to people I don't want to. This has been the high point of my night so far. Thank you."

"Same here," Gray said.

"Seriously, avoid the lobster roll." She said, eyes glimmering with playfulness.

"At all costs."

Gray watched Morgan flit through the room of people, like a bee from flower to flower.

Hoping to speak to her again, he waited around, forced to endure trifling conversations with boring people. That hope added to his overall confusion about the evening. The whole thing was childish and embarrassing. What if she did come back over to talk, he asked himself. What then? It wasn't like he had something to say. And why did he even want her to come back in the first place? She seemed kind, funny, easy to talk to, and welcoming. So why, he asked himself again, not wanting to acknowledge the truth.

The bee had stung him.

After not even coming close to speaking with Morgan again for an hour, Gray talked himself into leaving. He steered himself toward the door, navigating the hors d'oeuvres table on his route. Gray snatched a lobster roll and took a bite. Morgan was right. They were awful. Once outside the house, he spit the roll into the flowerbed.

~ ~ ~ ~

The Honda Accord sped along Interstate Four toward a black sky and a dark Gulf of Mexico. The billboards eased by, streetlight reflections glided across the windshield, and the car's tires produced a whirr of white noise. The collective effect created an environment that usually overpowered Gray's overthinking, resulting in Gray eventually pulling the car over wherever exhaustion took hold. Then he'd sleep. The nights when this didn't work, his unrelenting thoughts focused on the specifics of an investigation. To his recollection, never had Gray's overthinking centered on something like this, that made him feel good, that he hoped would happen again, but tonight Gray couldn't stop thinking about Morgan Beringer.

And he couldn't shake the confusion of it either.

CHAPTER 4

Consciousness arrived with the awareness of discomfort. Pain even. Nicole Abernathy shifted her body, wincing at the aching feeling but not opening her eyes, not fully conscious yet. It was an odd sensation to perform a body check while not awake, to have her brain working when her cognizance was shrouded in a thick fog. The sensation of pain became too prominent, and Nicole came to before completing the languid body check. The mental fog dissipated too quickly and was replaced by a disorienting sensation. Her eyelids lifted, seeing only darkness. Her mind swirled and a sudden release of panic and adrenaline choked her.

With darkness all around, she could hear branches of leaves rustling above her. Felt wetness underneath her, seeping through her clothes. Cars zoomed in the distance. Mosquitos buzzed near her ears. A cool breeze licked her skin. She forgot the pain as confusion and fear set in. Her respiring labored, like she was underwater and breathing oxygen through a straw.

Last she recalled she had been running. She'd been pushing her physical limits to reach the runner's high, when the world's problems melt away allowing her a few peaceful moments. Running, breathing, pacing. She remembered measuring her stride. Then ... Then ... Then she fell. Tumbled over and over, somersaulting, limbs striking wildly at the ground. She must've hit her head. She didn't remember much of anything else after that.

Lying on her back, Nicole's eyes cast into the sky and adjusted to the light of the moon above. It appeared, based on the amount of tree branches she saw between her and the moon that she wasn't near the running path, which was free of such cover. *How could that be?* Nicole sat up, ignoring the slight spinning of her head, and looked about. The moonlight wasn't strong enough to illuminate the entire surrounding area, but she didn't need the light in order to know now what had really happened to her, confirmed by the completion of a conscious body check. Her running shorts were twisted and bunched, and sat on her hips. Low on her hips. Her sports bra beneath her athletic shirt felt the same – bunched, not situated. Everything hurt. *Everything.*

She hadn't tripped and fallen. She hadn't somehow rolled via momentum this far away from the path. She'd been attacked. Anger, like she'd never experienced, erupted and made the pain go away. She pushed off the ground and stood, a strange heaviness tugging at her waist. She felt around, frantically swiping her hands here and there. *A chain!* Not only had she been raped, she'd been imprisoned here for a second go. She screamed for help, grabbing at the chain and pulling on it, hoping its bind wasn't secure. Unable to break it, she traced the chain's length, hand over hand, and found it hitched around a large oak's trunk. It was held there by a Masterlock. She desperately jerked the chain again, hoping against hope it would break.

"Help!" Her voice strained. "Someone help!"

No help came, though. Only the echoing of her pleas, and only faintly so.

Nicole then heard footsteps trudging through the woods. Funny, all she wanted was help, but the sound frightened her. She could hear the fear in her breathing, a hesitation of her lungs to let go of oxygen. Her jaw rattled in place, how it would if she were cold.

"Hello? Is someone out here?" she finally asked.

The male voice came to her through the darkness. "Who's there?"

"Here." Her voice broke. Fear and panic turned to relief and excitement. "I'm here. Help!"

"I'm coming."

The footsteps she heard had a quickened pace now. Help was on the way. Relief stole the strength from her legs, and Nicole fell to the ground, landing in a seated position. She held onto the chain with both hands. She didn't know why, but she did. Then she thought again about her new shoes, the promotion, her travel blog plans, and the new makeup she bought. How were these her first thoughts? She laughed at that their ridiculousness. Cried.

The footsteps stopped, bringing Nicole out of her head and delivering her eyes upward. A man stood before her. So happy to see him, she almost blurted out words of thanks. Yet, logic demanded that he'd be dressed as a runner, like her. She expected him to be someone who'd been running along the path and heard her cries for help. That wasn't the case.

A small lantern in his left hand showed that he was wearing work boots, jeans, and a long sleeve T-shirt instead of dri-fit clothes. The man's hands were covered with leather gloves. In his right, looped around his gloved forefinger swung a set of Masterlock keys.

"Nicole ... You're awake."

Horror invaded Nicole's mind. *He knows my name?*

"You were out of it when I left."

"Help!" She screamed as loud as she could, knowing there was only one way he knew her. "Help!"

Nothing mattered to her but getting out of there. She lifted the chain, somehow heavier now than before, and she thrust away from the man.

Forced into action by her screams, he pounced on her, knocking her onto her back. He covered her mouth, muffling any attempts at screaming.

"Shhh," he demanded.

He pushed his weight down on her face, forcing her head into the swampy ground. Realizing she couldn't match his strength, she complied and showed him as much by giving up her resistance. He held her there, though, enjoying the control over her again. His hands sealed her mouth closed. He knew she'd comply if for no other reason than oxygen. *Just like the rest.* He'd done this enough to know how to handle the situation. Some women fought, some fell paralyzed, while others went along with it. All of them, though, complied. Nicole was no different in the end.

"Don't scream again," he commanded, slowly letting off the pressure he'd been applying. He moved off her and stepped away. She stayed still and quiet. "Good."

The lantern, even though it had turned over, was bright enough for Nicole to see his arrogant smile. She instantly hated it, wouldn't forget it.

"You can sit up," he said, setting the lantern on its stand.

Hesitantly, she pulled herself together and shifted into a sitting position.

He rattled the keys in front of him. "I came to let you go."

Nicole knew he was playing with her, and she didn't like it. She extended the chain in front of her. "Then here. Unlock me."

He liked her spirit of defiance, but it didn't worry him. "We need to talk first."

"No, we don't," she said.

"I want you to know a few things."

"I don't care. If you're letting me go, then let's get on with it."

"You should care." He wrapped his fingers around the keys, enclosing them into a fist. She needed to know he controlled her destiny. He didn't *need* to let her go. He needed her to know that he *wanted* to let her go. While she watched the keys disappear into his gloved fist, he pulled with his other hand an object from his back pocket. The man moved directly into the lantern's cone of light.

"I know where you live."

It was her license. Nicole instinctively checked her tiny pocket. All its contents were gone.

"You have a nice place, Nicole. I'm very interested to see how successful your blog launch is. It's very exciting."

"I hate you."

"I'm not afraid to come see you again. Do you understand me?"

She did, but she didn't want to tell him. "Why did you do this?"

He had no desire to answer her questions. "Nicole, there's a slight likelihood you have vaginal tearing. For the next week or so, just keep yourself clean, try not to wear underwear, and no tampons."

"What?"

"Some bleeding is to be expected. I tried to be as gentle as I could."

Nicole scooted away from the man, taking her chain with her. She was glad she didn't recall what had happened to her, but that didn't mean she wasn't afraid of him.

"Best thing to do is go home, clean yourself up. If there is discomfort, use a heating pad or ice. Whichever feels better to you. I'd suggest ice or a cold compress."

"What makes you think I won't go straight to the police?"

"There's no need." He waited a moment for the best dramatic impact. "Rape kits are so unpleasant and demeaning. Besides, I wore a condom. There's no semen that'll be found. I'm completely shaved, so they'll find no loose hairs on you. I left no bite marks. I didn't kiss you, so no DNA can be swabbed from your mouth. And did you notice how wet your shorts are? And the ground around you? I already cleaned you up."

"They still might find something."

"They won't." He flashed that smile again. "Trust me."

She wondered how he could be so confident.

"You'd go through that invasive process for no reason."

Then it dawned on her. "You've done this before?" she asked.

He smiled, appreciative that she was keeping up with the conversation. "And mastered it, Nicole." He kept saying her name, reminding her of his control. "Plus ... " he pulled her cell phone from his pocket, "I've spent the last hour scrolling through your social media accounts." His tone turned conversational. "You know, it's still so surprising to me how many people in this day and age don't have passwords on their phones and they don't log out of the different accounts. People should think about their privacy and security.

"I mean, it didn't have to be me. Anyone could've snatched you up anywhere. Bottom-line is, bad people are everywhere, Nicole, and you don't want bad people to be able to see into your life. For instance, I know your favorite artist, TV show, movie, and book." He paused for affect. His tone threatening but calm. "I know who your family members are. And your friends." Another confident smile spread across his face. "So if you insist on going to the police and putting yourself needlessly through the rape kit process, I'll go see one of your family or friends and make them pay for your poor choices. Understand?"

She spoke through a clenched jaw. "Yes."

He decided to clarify. "You, I was nice to. I wasn't mad. It was just ... fun. You tell the police, and I'll be pissed. I'm not nice when I'm pissed."

"I said I understand." She stood, deciding it was the only thing she could do to show her strength. "All right?" She held up the chain again. "Unlock me."

CHAPTER 5

The unobstructed Florida afternoon sunshine zeroed in on the doorknob, and the nerves in Gray's hand were none too pleased about it when he turned the handle. The metal had heated to near burning temperatures. As Gray pulled the door open to Vandenhill's office, he noticed that the three large hibiscus plants, which had been blocking the door from the sun's heat rays, had been cut back by the lawn crew finishing up on the other side of the parking lot. Gray swiped his hand across his sport coat, trying to dull the pain the heated metal left on his skin, then he trudged up the stairs.

His morning had been shaken up and rearranged. Vandenhill had called and asked that he change his appointment time. The timeline adjustment forced him to rush the preparations for his next appointment with her. Gray had planned to run to the book store, purchase a travel book on Aruba, and read through the first few overview sections. That way he could show Vandenhill he was actively, willingly, and excitedly doing his homework. Though, he had no intention of going on vacation, but she didn't need to know that. With the change of plans, he had to rush to the store for the book, and he hadn't yet had time to read the overviews. That's what he planned on doing in the waiting room.

Realizing he was running out of reading time, his hurried up the stairs, taking two and three steps at a time. It made his entrance into Vandenhill's waiting room, quick, and abrupt.

The room contained a plastic potted plant in one corner, a small television set on top of a wicker end table, a couch, and a coffee table dotted with old magazines. The walls had framed prints of Monet's self-portrait and *Woman with Parasol in the Garden at Argenteuil*. Gray had never really paid attention to the room because it was always the same, because it just didn't matter to him, and because he was always alone in the room. The room was one of two Vandenhill had – an entry waiting room and an exit room. Since her therapy included many police cases – addiction, abused children and wives, sexual assaults, police officer counseling and the like – she didn't want her next appointment to see her previous appointment. Today apparently was different.

He paused when he entered the room because someone else was there as well. The young woman wore no makeup, had on workout clothes, and flip flops. Her hair pulled back in a bun. She seemed as startled to see him as he was to see her. The silence was so heavy that he thought maybe he was interrupting something, which was ridiculous because she was there alone.

"Sorry if I scared you," he said, watching her move away from him on the couch. "I kind of came rushing in, didn't I? Usually the room's empty."

She smiled politely but didn't respond.

"Do you mind?" Gray asked for permission to sit down, pointing to the couch cushion closest to him.

"Go ahead," she replied.

Her tone made her seem weak to Gray, and as he sat down, he thought he'd seen her try to move further away on the couch. He must've really scared her when he came in. Gray decided he'd leave her alone, and he thumbed through the Aruba book, hoping to finally prepare for the session.

The next couple minutes passed in silence. *An awkward silence*, Gray thought. He wasn't sure if the awkwardness was his issue or if it was simply an uncomfortable situation. Either way, when Vandenhill finally opened her office door, he was relieved but not as much as his couch-mate apparently. The woman in workout clothes hopped to attention, nearly jumping off the couch. She hurried to Vandenhill, who today was wearing navy blue slacks and a beige silk blouse. Usually she wore below the knee dresses.

"I'm sorry to keep you waiting," Vandenhill said.

Gray stood, partially to be a gentleman and partially because he expected to be quickly ushered into her office.

"It's okay," the woman replied.

Vandenhill folded a piece of paper in half and handed it to her. "This is the information I wanted you to take."

"Thank you."

"Call me if you need me."

"I will."

They hugged, which Gray thought was odd. He tried to stay out of their conversation, so he looked at the Monet prints on the wall instead. They seemed appropriate to Gray, like the only purposefully meaningful things in the waiting room. The impressionist's self-portrait lacked personal detail. You could see enough of the characteristics that you knew it was a face. A receding hairline and a Duck Dynasty beard, but that was about it. The rest you had to find yourself. Same with the other painting. The woman was standing among colorful, blooming flowers with what looked like a forested area behind her, like she was emerging from a world of known dangers into a world of beauty and clarity. Gray had never realized that before. Those prints illustrated the desired results of Vandenhill's therapy. She's letting you know before you enter her office what to expect. Gray looked back to the women embracing one another. He figured he was the self-portrait and the workout lady was the woman in the garden.

"I'll see you soon," Vandenhill said, breaking the embrace.

"Thank you."

The workout woman left and flip-flopped her way down the stairs.

"Sorry to keep you waiting, Becker."

After following Vandenhill into her office, Gray took his usual place in an oversized and over-cushioned Montclair accent chair. He held the Aruba travel book in front of him, waiting anxiously for her to see it and note that he'd completed his assignment. Instead she stood behind her desk, made a note on a pad of paper, clicked the pen, closed files, and shuffled them around. Seemingly unaware of him.

Gray accepted the silence for as long as he could. "I bought a book on Aruba. I think I'll go there on vacation."

Vandenhill didn't respond. She just kept moving files around. Finally, she opened one and pushed it away from her, almost to the edge of her desk which faced Gray. She sat down behind the desk. Slumped in her seat. Her eyes set on some faraway place, which apparently was where her mind had traveled as well.

Gray placed the book on the coffee table, nudging the melted-marble ashtray to the side. Annoyed now. "What's wrong?"

Vandenhill's eyes shifted, ascending to Gray's face. She sat up in attention quickly, seeming suddenly aware of his presence. In the same motion, she closed the folder that she'd pushed away from her. "You brought a book. Is that what you said?"

"You all right?" Gray asked rather than answering her question.

"Aruba?" Vandenhill asked.

Gray grabbed the book and showed her the cover.

Vandenhill clicked her pen and made a note on her pad. "Good, Becker. I'm glad you're considering vacation."

He placed the book on the table again. "You don't seem yourself. Should I come another time?"

Vandenhill considered Gray's question for a long time, at least that's what he thought she was thinking about. Then she asked, "How do you investigate a case?"

During their last session, Vandenhill asked Gray if he was suicidal, so he was used to her off the wall questions. This one, though, seemed different. "Methodically," he replied.

"Can you not just give straight answers?"

"Can you not ask such broad questions?" Gray snapped back at her.

With a grunt, she propped her elbow on the desk then rested her chin in the palm of her hand. Her eyes looked away again. Her mind drifted in thought. Gray let her go, content to let her wander for the moment. Besides, he had the time. Their hour had just begun. He thumbed through the Aruba book, sitting back in the chair.

Finally, she said, "I have a dilemma, Becker."

He put the book on the arm of the chair.

"About me?"

She made eye contact with him again. "No. Well … Yes."

He didn't think that sounded good.

"Spit it out."

She chewed on her cheek. "I have a patient who told me she was raped." Vandenhill fiddled with the pen in her hand. "It's not the first time I've heard a woman tell me that."

"Something's different this time?" He moved to the edge of his seat and leaned on his knees.

Vandenhill nodded. "One in six women in Florida have been raped. Did you know that?"

He knew that statistic.

"Over sixty percent of rapes are never reported."

He knew that one too.

"There's such a small likelihood of prosecution. And an even smaller chance the rapist will go to jail."

Gray had never seen her like this. She almost appeared distraught.

Her eyes focused on him again, bringing her thoughts back from wandering. "How was the holiday party at the mayor's house?"

Gray chuckled. "No segues today, doc?"

She smiled back. "Do I ever segue?"

"You click your pen."

"What?" She looked at the pen in her hand.

"When you're finished with a thought process, you click your pen."

Vandenhill placed the pen on her desk. "I didn't know I did that." She pushed the pen away from her, then, to keep Gray from reading her further, tucked her hands under her legs. "How was the party?" she asked again.

Gray didn't mind telling her about the pen clicking. He wanted her to know he watched her as closely as she watched him. He wanted her to know that he knew the way she was acting right now wasn't her norm. She needed to know she'd have to explain herself.

"It was nice. Not my crowd though."

"Did you meet Morgan Beringer?"

"The mayor's wife?" He played dumb, not wanting Vandenhill to pick up on how much he enjoyed meeting Morgan. "I did. Briefly."

"We're friends," she said.

"I didn't know that." An uneasiness washed over Gray.

"Have you ever broken the law during an investigation so you can catch a criminal?" she asked, leaning on the desk.

Enough was enough. Gray stood from the Montclair. "I don't know what's going on here. This isn't a normal session."

Vandenhill grabbed the pen that she had pushed away. "It's not, I know." She clicked the pen. "Please sit down."

"Whatever you're working through, I don't need to be a part of it."

She grunted again, frustrated at herself. She had tried to orchestrate the conversation, but it wasn't working and was losing him. "I think I need your help."

All but the Morgan question made sense to him then. "Is this about that girl in the waiting area? Was she the one who was raped?"

Vandenhill tossed the pen onto the desk and rubbed her face with her hands like she was scrubbing off her dilemma, then she stared at him for a long time, slumped down again in her seat. Gray wondered about her posture, as he sat down again. Vandenhill usually sat erect. That must've had everything to do with her thought process, usually straight as well. Today she slumped.

"Will you please just answer my question?" she asked.

"Sure."

"Have you ever broken the law in an investigation?"

"Maybe not the law, but I've broken the rules."

Vandenhill nodded, but it seemed to Gray to be a "thank you" for playing along.

"How was that for you? Did it work?"

"What question do you want me to answer?" he asked.

"Both."

"It worked," he said.

"And how was it for you?"

"How do you think it was for me?"

She sighed, annoyed. "Straight answers, Gray."

"Look, I don't know what's going on here, but I know you know me. How do you think it was for me? You know that answer."

"You didn't care because it worked."

"Exactly." Gray leaned his elbows on his knees. "Now let's stop with the cryptic questions and just tell me what's going on? That girl from the waiting room … Was she raped?"

"I'm struggling with the confidentiality of it all."

"No, you're not." Gray pushed off his knees and scooted to the seat's edge. "You've already decided or you wouldn't have brought all this up."

She sighed, giving up. "You're right." She broke eye contact with Gray as she collected her thoughts. "She was raped." Vandenhill tapped her finger on the folder nearest Gray. "These are my notes."

Gray pulled the folder off her desk, but he didn't open it. He was mad because Vandenhill was breaking her code of confidentiality and she had decided to include him in that without his permission. He wasn't sure he wanted to read the notes.

"I won't tell you her name, but she went for a run along the Fort Fraser Trail. You know where that is?"

Gray nodded. The Fort Fraser Trail stretched about eight miles from Bartow to Lakeland. Added to Florida's esteemed list of biking and hiking trails, amenities such as picnic areas, benches, and rest rooms were scattered along the path that meandered through wooded areas, fields and pastures, and groves of trees. It replaced an old train rail used for carrying citrus, and it commemorated the building in the 1830s of a U.S. Army post crucial in the Seminole Wars.

"She was pulled into the bushes and raped."

Gray's madness grew because he knew the answers to his questions but asked them anyway. "Did she report it? Did she go to the hospital or a clinic?"

"No. She went home and showered. She had to scrub him off of her."

"You know there's nothing I can do with this, don't you?" His agitation popped.

"The only reason I'm telling you about this is," she straightened her posture and rested her elbows on her desktop again, "there were others."

"What others?"

"I hear about rapes a lot. Three of them that I've heard about in the last four or five years seem ... connected."

Gray grinded his teeth as a way to control his anger. "I'm trying not to lose my temper."

"The circumstances of the attacks are different. One occurred in a car, one at a home, and this one along the trail. But the method of attack seems, at least, to be consistent. He comes out of hiding and strikes. Completely controls the women. In this latest attack, he tripped her while she was running. He knocked her out, chained her to a tree, then raped her. She doesn't remember the attack, but, like the others, he explained to her why he wouldn't get caught. He takes precautions so as not to leave trace evidence behind. He lets them know he's been perfecting his skills for a long time and there's no reason to report the crime."

Gray realized he wouldn't have to read Vandenhill's notes because she was forcing them onto him. He tossed the folder on top of the Aruba travel book and the ashtray.

"Then comes the threats, just in case the woman is still thinking about reporting the crime. The threat seems to be his signature because it's consistent across all the women's versions of the attack.

"He learns about the girl through her social media presence. I don't get the impression he picked any of them through social media. More of a controlling tool after the fact. In this case, he used the woman's phone to access her accounts. Social media, it's like an open-access listing of your every like and dislike, every interest, and every friend or associate you have. He learns where she lives. Where she works. Where her families are. I mean, just about everything about any person is on social media. He threatens to attack one or more of her friends or family. He has their names too, and all the same information about them. All from her social media access. Thus completes the circle of control. Not to mention, the additional and scarier threat is of him coming back and doing this again whenever he wants.

"In this latest attack, he found the woman's license and keys, then he went to her apartment. He found her cell. It was unlocked and her accounts were set to stay logged in. He learned all about her. Her favorite songs, movies, and books. Her favorite restaurant, where she's vacationed. If she's married or single. When her birthday is. I mean, just about everything you could want to know about someone."

"Then he just lets them go?"

"He's confident in his process. It must work."

"All three of them, the same thing?" Gray asked, completely irritated that her approach worked, that he fell for it.

"Same knowledge of the victim, same threat to her and her friends."

"She has to report it."

"She won't," Vandenhill said.

"She has to. I can't do anything with it without saying you told me."

"You can't do that!"

"I should." Gray spoke with a stern tone.

"I only told you because there were others." She thought that was justification enough, but she added more. "One was a patient. I won't tell you her name either. The other is my friend, who told me about this outside the doctor-patient relationship."

"Not one of them reported it?" His tone cut at her. "You couldn't get one of them to call it in?"

"No, I did. My other patient reported it, but her attacker kept his promise and went to visit her again. And one of her friends. She quickly retracted the report."

"And the friend didn't report it either?"

"I doubt it."

"Damn it."

"At least, not that I know of."

"Do you know her name?" Gray asked.

"No."

Gray's adrenaline fueled his thoughts which were shooting in a hundred different directions. Most directions led to anger about being manipulated by Vandenhill. Because of their sessions, she knew he'd fixate on this, drive himself crazy with it, and he'd ultimately keep her secret.

"You've given me nothing here." Frustration swelled and forced Gray into a pacing stride. "What am I supposed to do with this?"

Vandenhill got to her feet too. She rushed around her desk and grabbed the folder off the coffee table. "Take the folder. Read it. You have to be able to find the report the first girl placed. There's got to be a record of it somewhere."

He snatched the folder from her hands. "And then what? How do I justify looking for that particular report? How do I justify looking into the crime?"

"Make something up! You said you've broken the rules before. Break them again."

That froze Gray's stride. His anger rose front and center. "You set me up."

"I didn't." Vandenhill took a step back, seeing the anger in his eyes.

"Yes, you did." Gray dropped the folder on the table again. "This is what's going to happen." He pointed his finger at her. "You and I are done, but you're going to sign off on any of my departmental psych evals that may come your way. You got it? I'll never be back in here. We'll never talk again. You'll doctor the reports like I did come in, like we did talk, and you'll approve each and every one of them."

"I can't do that, Becker. You've come such a long way. There's still more you can do, if you'll keep coming to session."

Gray pointed his finger at her again. His fury penetrated her eyes.

"All right. Fine," she said, which lowered his finger and eased the tone of his glare. "If I do that, will you investigate this?"

Gray shook his head, suddenly tired. "I don't know."

"I mentioned a friend of mine. This happened to her, too. She's not a patient, like I said. Maybe you could talk to her. Maybe she'd finally come forward and report the crime."

"I don't know," Gray said again.

"It was Morgan Beringer," Vandenhill said. She hoped the name would pack a punch for Gray. She bet that Gray's brief encounter meant more to Gray than he said it did. She knew anyone who met Morgan fell for her instantly. Gray couldn't be any different, she hoped.

"The mayor's wife?"

"Yes."

His breath caught, realizing why when she first asked about Morgan she didn't click her pen. He instantly hated the rapist. He instantly grew confused about Morgan and how she could live with such a secret? And what about her husband, Douglas? He used to be a cop. How could he allow his wife to not report the crime?

Vandenhill took Gray's shock as confirmation that he'd fallen a bit for Morgan. Morgan was a flirt. She was attractive, fun, intelligent but down to earth and humble. She appealed to all types of men. Gray was no exception, Vandenhill was happy to note in this case. She instinctively wrapped her fingers around her pen and clicked it twice.

The clicking snapped Gray from his thoughts, and he glared at Vandenhill again.

She knew Gray wouldn't tell anyone what she'd told him, and she hoped Morgan would forgive her. "He's going to keep doing this, Becker."

CHAPTER 6

Gray had taken from Vandenhill's office the folder containing her notes about the alleged rape. He read through them before he'd even left her building's parking lot. Probably according to her plan. The way she used him – played him, really – left him infuriated, but he convinced himself she was acting with the best of intentions. He wondered, too, if he'd reacted too heavy-handed with her, demanding she falsify his paperwork. That didn't matter now. He shook off those thoughts because it was done. She got what she wanted and so had he, he guessed. Some would say that was a win-win situation.

He called his partner, Jeffrey Parker, and arranged to meet for an early lunch. The hostess at the chain restaurant sat Gray in a booth where he waited for Parker to arrive. Gray ordered two waters and by the time the waitress delivered them Parker walked through the doors. Gray waved him over.

"I'm not fitting in that thing." Parker was a large man. Six and half feet and about 300 pounds. He wore a dress shirt and tie. No jacket today.

"How about a table?" Gray asked the waitress.

"Or anywhere with more room than that booth. It's like a thimble."

After they were situated at a four-top table, Parker ordered an iced tea and reviewed the menu. "How'd the head shrinking go today?"

Gray waved off the question.

"All right," Parker said. "Take two: how about the holiday party at the mayor's?"

Spotting the waitress heading back to the table, Gray asked, "Do you know what you want to eat?"

"Of course." Parker smiled such as to tell Gray he had asked a dumb question.

They ordered – Gray a tilapia with rice, Parker a burger with broccoli as a side.

"I'll try for a third question and see if you answer that."

"Oh, the party." Gray had hoped Parker would let the subject go. "The party was fine. The mayor and his wife were nice, but the rest was everything you know I hate."

"Small talk and people."

"Pretty much."

Parker laughed, amused by Gray's reluctance or unwillingness to be friendly.

"Have you ever wondered," Parker asked, "why we're friends? Or how we became friends?"

"No," Gray said and gulped his water.

Parker leaned in toward Gray and spoke softly so no one except Gray would hear him. "How was she?"

"Who?"

"The mayor's wife?"

"What are you talking about?" Gray was instantly defensive. He was unsure if he was defensive for himself or for her. He didn't want anyone to know he couldn't stop thinking about her, and he didn't want anyone to attack her. That had already happened to her, according to Vandenhill.

A long time ago Parker began ignoring Gray's responses. Or their tone, rather. Parker had always believed that it wasn't what you said to a person but how you said it. Except when it came to Gray. To understand Gray, you had to apply the rule in reverse. Most of the time it wasn't how he said something but what he said that was important.

"I've always heard she is gorgeous. I mean, I've seen pictures of her, and she looks amazing. Is she the same in person? Or better? Oh, don't tell me she's better." By the time he was finished talking, his voice was back to normal volume.

"I didn't notice, Jeff."

"Bullshit, you didn't notice." His voice was loud this time.

Gray scanned the room. No one seemed to hear Parker despite the volume of his protest.

"I didn't notice. There's nothing wrong with that. Besides, who cares?"

"You noticed." Parker said it like it was fact. "Her husband's a lucky man."

"Okay." Gray wasn't going to talk about her husband, still upset about him not making his wife report the rape. "How's your wife?"

"What?" Parker said. "Karen? She's awesome. We went to the beach last weekend. You know, after all these years, she still can pull off a mean bikini."

"You're clearly juiced on Viagra today."

Parker chuckled at Gray's quip. "Maybe. I am extra amped. I have another meeting with Cannon today."

The food came before the conversation could continue. Parker tore into his burger. Gray forked his fish and pushed the rice around the plate, realizing the importance of the subject Parker had just mentioned.

"About the cold case unit that she's putting together?" Gray asked, quickly formulating a plan of how to use the conversation.

Cannon was Lieutenant Lexie Cannon. She was in the running for the next Chief of Police, if and when Reginald Boudreaux ever retired or was terminated. She'd been with the department for so long, no one knew for sure how long.

Parker grunted a response, nodded, then wiped his mouth with a napkin. He didn't speak until he'd finished chewing his food. "It's a bit of a shit show right now."

"How so?" Gray asked.

"Everything takes money, right? The department isn't getting more of a budget from the city for this, but you need money to implement a new unit. So where's it coming from?"

"I don't know," Gray replied, wanting to encourage Parker to continue talking.

"Cannon's idea is to take the money from West's gang team?"

The internal politicking on this was apparent even to Gray, who normally paid no attention to that sort of thing. Lieutenant Lexie Cannon had been campaigning to the budget committee to split – what she called – the "ridiculous" amount of allocated funds that went to the gang and organized crime division ran by Sergeant Maxine West. Cannon explained that the money would be reallocated to a cold case team. Based on the rumors that circulated after the last committee meeting, West had agreed to take a partial hit to her budget but explained that the whole funding for the cold case unit shouldn't come from only her budget. She suggested every business unit should take a percentage hit – 10-20% – to fund the new squad. That seemed like a better solution than only shrinking her team's budget.

"West won't let that happen," Gray said

West, while not as high ranking as Cannon, was a supremely respected member of the police department. Her team did great work, and gave Boudreaux reason after reason to call the press together touting his department's successes. Therefore, Cannon and West were both accustomed to getting what they wanted, but one of them this time wouldn't.

"We'll see." Parker took another bite of his burger. "Why?"

Gray shrugged his shoulders as if to say, "No reason." But Gray had a reason for prolonging that topic of conversation. And for where he'd take it. He wondered how natural the gesture looked. Parker was a detective after all and knew when people were lying.

"I was just curious."

Gray realized he was playing with the pepper shaker. *Did Parker see that?* He wondered if this was his version of Vandenhill clicking her pen. The mental comparison to Vandenhill hit him hard. He was doing the same thing to Parker that she'd done to him just an hour ago. He didn't like himself for it.

"They'll need a sergeant to run that unit," he continued. "Will you put in for it?"

"You want to get rid of me?" Parker objected in a joking manner.

"You said something last year about wanting to get promoted. I was just asking. You're on Cannon's cold case committee. Seems to me like you have an inside shot at running the unit."

Parker sucked down half the glass of iced tea, shaking his head while he did it. "Not right now," he said. "Why? Do *you* want to put in for it?" Parker asked.

Gray scoffed at the idea, shaking his head. "No. I'm good right where I am." Gray preferred his position as one of the lead detectives in the major crimes unit. That's where he could do the best work. Besides, he was no administrator. "When are they planning to make a decision?"

Frustration immediately showed on Parker's face. "I don't know. You know nothing moves fast here. It's a political bullshit rodeo. I have friends in the Philadelphia PD who talk about the crap going on behind the scenes there. You know, big city, big budget, big crime. Politicians there hoping to eventually be the governor and all that. It's awful. But here ... Look, Lakeland is great. I've been here, what? Five years? Something like that. It's a cool place. People are friendly. They kind of got that southern hospitality thing going on. Small town feel. People waving to each other when they drive by. All of that. But it's not a small town. I guess you expect some politicking, but ... I don't know, man. This whole good ol' boy network ... It's alive and well. I'll tell you that."

That was more of a response than Gray expected. He ignored the parts that didn't interest him. "They talked about this unit before. Long time ago. Before you were here. They found the remains of a woman out by the railroad tracks off of Main Street. Way out past that lumber company that's out there. I can't remember the name of it. They make pallets and stuff. I can't remember. That case generated talk about a cold case unit. Nothing came of it though."

"Man, with the way talks are going now, a case that generated more momentum for a cold case unit would be good for Cannon and bad for West. That's for sure."

"Right." That's what Gray wanted. *Seed planted*, he thought.

Parker pushed his plate away during the pause in conversation. "You want dessert?"

"Do you?"

Parker shrugged his shoulders, which Gray knew meant he did want dessert. "Only if you're having some."

"I'll have coffee while you have dessert. They have good carrot cake here," Gray said.

"And some ice cream. That sounds good."

CHAPTER 7

Dusk approached. The heat was subsiding, and the mosquitos would start buzzing soon. The humidity, though, wouldn't relent for another few months. If Florida was lucky enough for a hurricane to form in the Atlantic Ocean and it not make landfall, then the weather system would pull the moisture from the air and Florida would be left with hot days and little-to-no humidity. Strange how a dry 95 degrees could be something to look forward to.

The large oak and camphor trees acted as a canopy and made it appear later in the evening than it was. Gray sat in his police cruiser five doors down from Douglas and Morgan Beringer's home. The mayor would be at his monthly town hall meeting, so Gray knew he'd be able to meet with Morgan without Douglas being present, if she was home. He knew having her alone and to himself would be best for the task at hand. He thought the same way for personal reasons. He shook his head at the foolishness of these personal reasons. He hadn't thought about a woman in this way for an extremely long time. Why now? Why the mayor's wife? And why did she have to be a victim in a case he wanted to investigate?

Gray had been in his car on the Beringer's residential street for almost 30 minutes, and he still hadn't figured out how he would approach the topic of her rape. The car was running and the air conditioning was blasting at half power. He watched the house, noting only one room's light burning. Then he heard the knock on his passenger window. He turned quickly, his hand instinctively moving toward his weapon, and saw Morgan. No makeup, hair back in a bun, sweaty, skin reddened by exertion. Smiling.

His hand relaxed, and Gray rolled down the window, greeted her.

"I hope this isn't your surveillance car, detective. I could tell it was a cop car a mile away."

He was embarrassed. He hoped it didn't show.

"It's not, but noted for future reference." He smiled, mirroring her lightheartedness again. "I was hoping to visit a minute."

"Speaking of a mile away, did you forget where the house is?" She pointed down the street.

Gray decided to go with it, since he had no better alternatives.

"Embarrassingly, yes, I did."

She didn't know if she believed him. "Douglas is at a town hall meeting tonight." She wiped sweat off her face then dried her fingers on her shorts.

"I meant with you actually."

She laughed, maybe embarrassed herself. "I'm quite smelly and a bit of a mess right now."

"I don't mind. I think it's important."

"All right then." She smiled again. "Unlock the door. I'll ride with you to the house."

"It's against department policy to transport smelly women."

She snickered, amused but acting as if she wasn't. "Unlock the door."

Gray did, and Morgan hopped into the car.

"Roll up the window and turn off the air. I want you to get the full experience."

Gray laughed. "I don't think so."

"Your punishment for coming over unannounced is to ride in a sealed car with me. Now drive."

Not only could she dress to the nines beautifully, she could also be one of the boys. He liked that.

"Just promise to take the wheel if I pass out."

She laughed and slapped Gray on the arm.

~ ~ ~ ~

Once inside the house, she asked for a moment to wash up. Gray didn't think she was taking a shower, but Morgan ran up to her bedroom after pouring a glass of water for herself and for Gray. Gray swallowed the chilled beverage that had a hint of mint and cucumber infused. He held in a quiet panic because he still didn't know what he was going to say to her. Normally, he'd have the conversation mapped out, but this time was different. Worse, he was nervous. As if that wasn't enough to process, he didn't see Morgan as a victim. She was strong and confident. No pain visible at all – external or internal. No signs of victimization. It confused him. Or, was it the way he thought of her that was confusing him?

"Thank you," she said, entering the kitchen. She looked as if she'd washed her face. She wore a different workout outfit than before. Gray thought he caught a trace of perfume as well.

"No worries."

Morgan moved quickly to the refrigerator and pulled out the jug of the infused water, cheese cubes, and a colander of grapes. "Snack, detective?" She arranged it all on the island countertop separating them.

"Thanks."

She handed him a plate and spoon to dish out the grapes and cheese.

"And I thought we were going by first names. Did you forget mine, Mrs. Beringer?"

"No, Becker. Did you forget mine?"

He wanted to say that he'd never forget it, but instead he said, "I remember."

"Then it depends on why you're here." She tossed a cheese cube and two grapes into her mouth.

"Probably more business than pleasure unfortunately."

"Then detective it is."

Gray hated what he was about to do. They'd likely not have these playful discussions any longer.

"What is it?" she asked, catching him in thought.

"Sorry," Gray replied, brushing aside his distracting thoughts. "The department is looking to fund a rape support group, and I thought I'd ask you if you'd be involved. You know, the mayor's wife supporting women's issues. I thought it'd give the group instant credibility."

He didn't like lying to her. He liked it less when he saw her subtly pull back from him. She hid it well, but Gray saw it. *The moment their relationship died.*

"I don't do things like that, detective. The limelight, if you will, isn't my thing. I'm sure Douglas will support it." She sealed the bag of cheese cubes. "Besides, there's already a very good support group for that, and I believe it works best out of the public eye."

"I understand."

She retrieved Gray's plate. "Is that all you wanted, detective?"

He knew she was excusing him, shutting him out. He had to be less subtle. "There's a woman who was recently attacked. She was clubbed and knocked out, dragged into the woods, chained to a tree. Raped repeatedly. Then the man used her social media accounts to learn more about her and her friends. He threatened to come back and rape her again, if she reported the crime. He also threatened to randomly pick one of her social media friends and rape her too. She hasn't reported the crime yet, so there's not much we can do to help her."

Morgan's face locked, showing only slight fury. "Let's hope she comes forward then." Morgan haphazardly returned the food and water to the refrigerator. She took Gray's plate and glass and placed them in the kitchen basin.

"If there's nothing else, detective." She held her arm out toward the front door.

"She's too afraid to come forward, but we believe there are other victims, and we'd like your help."

"Goddammit. I've been nice. Now it's time for you to go."

Gray held his arms up, indicating he was surrendering.

"Please leave." Morgan was on the verge of tears.

Gray followed her to the front door. Her body movement was stiff, not like at the party when she flitted around like a bee. As they reached the door, Gray was surprised when she stopped, seemed to freeze, and didn't open it. More surprised when she spun around. Fury had clearly taken root on her face. She lashed out, slapping Gray. Then she pushed him backward with both of her hands. Gray stumbled backward, not yet feeling the sting of the slap, concentrating more on his footing.

"Who told you?"

She pushed him again.

"I said, who told you?"

Following the force of her last strike, Gray's retreat was halted by the bannister of the stairs. She tried to lash out again, but Gray caught her by the arm, stopping the attack. His response snapped her out of her furious episode and brought her back to reality. He released her arm as quickly as he caught it. She stepped backward, avoiding eye contact. He didn't know if she just didn't want to face him or if she wanted to hide her release of tears. As she hurried into the kitchen, the sting of her slap finally took root on Gray's cheek.

He found Morgan leaning on the island. Her head hung low in her attempt to hide her crying. Gray hated seeing her like that. He hadn't liked lying to her either. He again reminded himself of Vandenhill. All of the conversations he took part in lately were agenda-driven and manipulative.

"Would you like to talk about it?"

Morgan reared her head. "No, I don't want to fucking talk about it."

"We need help finding this guy."

"And yet you keep talking."

Gray waited a beat before continuing. "He's attacked four women that I know of. There's more, I'm sure, and I know he'll keep doing it."

"I know it's selfish, but that's not my problem."

She moved away from the counter and washed her face in the sink. Gray waited as she dried her face. The kitchen looked like it came right out of an Ikea catalog. Everything had a place in the neatly designed room, appliances strategically placed across the granite countertops. Morgan tossed the hand towel on the counter. It butted up against a loaded knife block.

"It's not selfish, but it's also not the only way to handle this."

"Douglas doesn't know. I never told him."

Gray nodded, realizing this complicated the situation greatly. Morgan telling her husband could send this situation in a thousand different directions. Gray had hoped to keep a lot of what he was doing quiet, kind of sneak it in. Her husband's potential reaction could jeopardize that. With the power in the city he had, this could blow up in Gray's face. Then he shook aside the thoughts. None of that was his problem. Not really. He could handle the blow up. He'd handled them before, and he'd never been afraid to push the limits. Ultimately, he wanted to catch the rapist and put a stop to his activity, yes, but there was something else at play here too. Something new. Something that wasn't there when he parked down the road from the house. As he finally saw Morgan's vulnerability, he wanted her to be healed more so than catching her rapist.

"I'll find another way," Gray said.

His words pulled her out of her thoughts again. They seemed to calm her, but they didn't wash away her pain.

"Who told you?" she asked.

He thought about not telling her the truth, but he didn't want to lie to her again. "Frances Vandenhill."

Morgan nodded, processing that information. Gray wondered if she felt betrayed and if by telling her he had ruined their friendship.

"Then I know she had a good reason."

She surprised Gray again. This time with her forgiveness. Maybe that's something she learned during her recovery from the rape. Gray had heard that before from victims – that forgiveness gave them strength.

"What else did she tell you?" Morgan asked.

"She stuck to the facts. Nothing personal."

"Nothing is more personal than being raped!"

The outburst unsettled Morgan. She leaned on the counter, hoping not to cry again, struggling to control her anger.

He wanted to apologize, but it wasn't appropriate.

"I'm sorry I slapped you," she said.

Gray realized the stinging in his cheek had faded.

In a single flowing movement, she pushed herself off the counter and leaned against the sink behind her. She breathed in deeply and exhaled slowly, still composing herself. Gray took note that the movement also created more space between them.

"I haven't told anyone other than Frances, and then hearing you talk about it … I guess," she held her hands in front of her like she was holding a ball, "my world imploded for a moment." She brought her hands together and interlocked her fingers, as if crushing the imaginary ball.

"What happened?" Gray asked. But not to convince her to cooperate. He cared.

By the look on her face, she wasn't expecting that question. Or maybe she didn't want to answer it.

"Would you like some coffee or tea?"

"Sure. Coffee please."

Morgan smiled, Gray figured, liking the idea of movement. Avoiding the question a few moments longer, Morgan used a Kuerig machine and brewed Gray a cup of Columbian coffee and herself a cup of green tea. They stayed quiet through the process.

"Thanks." Gray took the cup from her.

Morgan held her cup with both hands, finding comfort in the heat. She brought it close to her face and breathed in the scent. Finally, she said, avoiding eye contact and looking to the floor like the memory was at her feet, "It was about a year and a half ago and very much like you described. He threatened my friends, and I believed him." She thought more before speaking. "That's about all I want to recount of it." Her eyes raised from the floor to Gray.

"How have you not told Douglas?"

She shrugged her shoulders. "I used to face things head on … now I don't."

She sipped her tea. Gray followed suit with his coffee. Afterward she held onto her cup and Gray set his on the counter in front of him. He was going to ask her another question, but she started talking.

"Douglas knows something is different. That's what hurts the most." Her voice cracked with emotion. "He thinks I've pulled back from him because of something he's done." The emotional fight inside her almost prevailed against her strength. "He tried for a long time to … I don't know … pull me back to him, I guess. Now he doesn't even try. He's paying a punishment for all of this, too."

Morgan's words halted Gray. This whole situation wasn't what he had expected. He'd thought Morgan had told her husband who then had forced her to stay quiet for the sake of his political career. He thought Douglas had betrayed his law enforcement background simply to win an election. Gray thought he would convince her easily to come forward and help the investigation. He thought he understood his attraction to her. But none of that was happening.

Morgan's past was echoing back at her, and Gray had stepped into the picture to unbox it, sending the memories soaring chaotically into Morgan's life like a tornado of painful and destructive shrieking. Shrieking that would eventually pierce every component of the world Morgan had built for herself – her marriage, her family, her friends, her reputation, her social standing. He hated that he'd been the one to unleash that. Worst, his attraction to her made him weak. He normally would push forward and ignore all of that to solve the case. This was different. The pain in her eyes meant something. Rather, it meant something *to him*. He wanted to hold her and comfort her.

"I can't report the crime, Becker. It would destroy Douglas."

Gray used his index finger and pushed the handle of the coffee cup in a circle, thinking of how to respond. His thoughts spun like the cup. Only faster. His original intent in coming to her house needed to be recalibrated. His desire to comfort her needed to be tamed.

With his thoughts finally collected, he said, "This may overstep the bounds of our relationship, but it seems like maybe not reporting the crime is destroying Douglas … and more. Maybe even you."

Pondering that, Morgan took another deep breath and a mouthful of her tea.

"I'm not here," Gray said continued, "to judge, Morgan. I'm not even here anymore to ask you to come forward, and I'm the last person who can give any type of relationship advice, but … you should tell Douglas. Give him a reason to fight for you."

Morgan exhaled. It came out like a long, slow sigh, a breath of relief, of relenting, of accepting what needed to be done. However, her silence left Gray thinking there was a battle going on between her mind and her heart.

Gray took a final gulp of coffee. He set the cup down and spun it in a circle with his index finger again. He tried to figure out if there was anything left to say. He looked away from the cup and saw she was looking again at the floor. He studied her face, noticed the light hue of pink that nature had painted on her lips. Then he wondered if he would ever see her again after he left.

He spun the cup one last time, then finally apologized. "I'm sorry I brought this to you, Morgan."

His words for a third time pulled her from her thoughts. *You didn't.* She smiled, warmth attached to it. "And to think I was excited to see you."

He appreciated her attempt at playful deflection, which convinced him that he would never see her again. "I should go."

She set her cup down in agreement then led him toward the front door. Gray watched her move gracefully in front of him and wished the path to the door was a longer walk. She pulled the door open but blocked the doorway, looked up at him, started to say something, but then stopped. Morgan didn't know how to say what she felt. Gray had visited for his own purposes, but he was leaving having tried to help her. She appreciated that.

"Are you all right?" Gray asked.

"I don't know," she said, wanting to embrace him, to be comforted by someone who knew about her pain.

"I'm sorry about all this."

Morgan raised her arms and pulled him into a hug. He was stiff at first, but the embrace was warm and became more natural the longer it lasted. Gray found himself wrapping his arms around her. Stray hairs which had escaped her bun tickled the side of his face. Her arms held onto him as tight as his to her.

"Thanks," she said.

The embrace finally broke, and their eyes held for a short moment.

"We're letting in the mosquitoes." He ushered past Morgan. "Let me know if I can help." He knew she wouldn't call.

She closed the door behind him, and Gray stepped off the front step. "Shit," he said to himself, knowing he may have left the case inside the house during a moment of weakness.

CHAPTER 8

He had driven his Accord until he could hardly stay awake. Images of Morgan Beringer played in Gray's mind as he stumbled off to sleep, a process that was never smooth, never gentle, and never restful. The images had been the catalyst for the kind of night when his consciousness never seemed to turn off. Thoughts and dreams – he hardly ever dreamed – invaded his sleep to the point he knew he had slept but it felt like he was awake all night. The thoughts were random and disconnected from reality, and they left no distinct memory. However, his dream was different. He dreamt of fire whose smoke billowed high into a purple sky. The smoke gathered, trapped under a canopy of long branches, lush with large leaves. He couldn't see the trunk of the trees, just the outstretched branches full of leaves. The pungent vapor accumulated so thick in that canopy that finally the leaves began crumpling and dying. They turned a shade of blue that Gray had never seen before, then they turned brown and black, strangled. Soon they broke off from the branch. One then ten then hundreds. They floated, lightly making their way toward their fate, the fire. More smoke puffed upward, sending the leaves in all directions, yet never soaring far from the fire's gravitational pull.

To Gray, it appeared as if the fire was toying with the leaves. Pulling and pushing them. Using them for its own purpose.

Gray woke, feeling more tired than when he'd went to sleep. He rubbed the night from his eyes, and he expected the dream to wipe away with the crusty sleep. The dream stuck with him though. He wondered what happened to the smoke that had strangled the leaves and broken them off the branches. Had all the leaves fallen and the smoke continued to rise, escaping into the purple sky? He pushed off the side of his bed, wondering why it mattered.

Coffee in each hand, Gray fumbled with his entry into the Lakeland Police Department building. He took the stairs to the Major Crimes office and plopped into his desk chair. It didn't appear as Parker had arrived yet, so Gray looked through the files on his desk, phone messages, and logged on to his computer to check email. Before the device had booted to its desktop, Parker abruptly entered the office. It reminded Gray of the Kool-Aid guy, bursting into a room through walls. It was that abrupt. Parker's face held the excitement of a child.

"Thank God." Parker reached over Gray to grab one of the cups of coffee.

Gray stopped him. "Wait. Those are mine."

"What? Both?" Parker asked, pulling back his arm.

"I'm really tired today."

Parker studied Gray. "Are you kidding? You went to the coffee shop on your day to buy coffee, ordered two coffees, and one of them isn't for me?"

"Is every day my day to buy coffee?" Gray protested.

"Jesus, Becker. If you ever bought coffee, then it wouldn't be your day."

Parker sat in his desk chair. His cubicle was next to Gray's. He swiveled in the chair toward Gray and scooted closer. Gray noticed the file in his hands.

"Oh … Well, I'd give it to you, but I drank out of both already."

"You drank out of both? What kind of animal are you?"

Gray shrugged his shoulders. "They're both mine. I wasn't thinking."

Parker shook his head, annoyed but not truly surprised at the situation. "Walk with me." Parker held up the file in front of him.

"Where?"

Parker stood. "The kitchen. I want some coffee."

Gray locked his computer, grabbed his two cups, and followed Parker out the office door. By then Parker was already half way down the hall. Gray took a gulp of coffee from the cup in his left hand before picking up his pace. He entered the kitchen as Parker slammed the file down onto the counter.

"It's still brewing," he said, looking at Gray as if to blame him.

"We can wait." Gray swallowed coffee from the cup in his right hand. "What's in the file?"

Parker looked around the kitchen. Empty. He hurried around Gray and checked the hallway, clearly not wanting anyone to hear their conversation. Parker stood in the kitchen's doorway so he could check the hallway during the conversation to know when someone was coming toward them.

"An anonymous tip made its way to Lieutenant Cannon. A cold case. Kind of."

While listening to Parker, Gray poured the coffee from his two cups into the kitchen sink and threw the cups into the trash bin.

"What do you mean by *kind of*?"

Parker checked the hallway again. All clear. "According to the tip, three years ago a man raped a woman named Melanie Hyde. He threatened her by using her social media presence. Said he would rape one of her online friends if she reported the crime. She reported it. Then she pulled the report and stopped cooperating. The case died. Assuming one of her friends was raped too."

"All of that was in the tip?" Gray asked, pouring himself a fresh cup of coffee from the pot that finished brewing. He doctored it with cream and sugar.

"It was. And … the tip was generally telling us that he'd started up again. Same MO used recently. But the woman won't come forward because of the threat. And there are others. But that information wasn't included. Maddy James is pulling the old case files to see if there's any evidence that may help us. I have the report here from the original complaint."

"Sounds like there's enough there to start with." Gray tasted the hot coffee.

"You asshole." Parker stormed past Gay to the coffee pot and poured his own cup.

"Oh, I forgot. Sorry."

"You didn't forget. You're just an asshole." The frustration was real, tinged with friendship. But real.

"I was listening intently to you and forgot. Gimme a break."

Parker turned. "What is it with you and bringing me coffee? We skip days. I buy one day, you buy the next. I thought that's the system, but you never seem to follow it."

Gray shrugged his shoulders. "I forget."

Parker shook his head at Gray and sipped his coffee, returning to the doorway. He checked the hall. Still all clear. He wanted to finish the conversation since he figured whoever brewed the pot of coffee would be returning soon for their own cup.

"Cannon thinks this could be the case to help build more momentum for her cold case unit. She wants us to look into it."

"What?" Gray's face registered a lack of interest. "I have other things I need to do. I have a court date in a couple days. I was going to review my notes and the case files today."

"Forget that … like it's my coffee. No big deal. You'll get caught up one way or the other."

Gray poured out the coffee in the kitchen sink and tossed the cup.

"What are you doing?"

"Too much sugar."

"See. Now I know you're messing with me." Parker shook his head again, then got back to business. "Ride with me."

CHAPTER 9

Originally built in the 1920s by a combination of two natural keys and dredged mud from Tampa Bay, Davis Islands was supposed to be developed into an exclusive resort destination. Now it mainly contained residential structures, some so expensive only the highest paid sports stars could afford to live there. A few structures erected from the original plan for the islands still existed, as did, Gray presumed, a couple other island life essentials, like naming nearly every street on the islands after bodies of water and not installing any traffic lights.

Parker drove the cruiser from Hyde Park Avenue, over the bridge, and merged onto Davis Boulevard. Their GPS guided them past what looked like the only two blocks of restaurants, shops, and pubs on the islands, and told them to cut left onto Chesapeake and then right on Channel Drive where the view beyond a tree-lined road included Tampa General Hospital, those expensive houses, and a shipyard and its field of oil tanks.

Out of the parked car, Parker stretched and took in the view. The fishy smell of the ocean and the exhaust from a ship across the channel burned his nose. "I thought the view would've been nicer for some reason."

Gray pushed his car door closed and adjusted his holster. He didn't look at the channel. The house where they'd parked had caught his attention. Spanish-styled – as was the intent of the islands' founder D. P. Davis' planned resort – and massive, Gray figured the place was 20 times the size of his apartment.

"She lives here?" he asked Parker. "You sure?"

Parker checked the file he still clung to, which contained all of the information surrounding Melanie Hyde's alleged rape including her last known address.

"That's what the DMV thinks."

"Her name's Hyde?" Gray turned to Parker, and he noticed a small lighthouse positioned at the tip of the other island, which was called Little Grassy Key before Davis purchased it. "We just drove through Hyde Park. You think that's a coincidence?"

"Was Hyde Park named after someone?" Parker rounded the car and stopped at Gray's side. The coffee he'd drank on the way to Tampa from Lakeland had kicked in and he finally felt awake.

"I don't know. I assume so. These islands were."

Parker knocked on the front door of the house. The entry way was tiled and two steps led to the double front doors which rose 20 feet. A girl of about 15 years opened the one of the doors. Instantly the scent of lavender poured out of the house. It smelled better than the aromas blowing in from the channel.

"Hi, we are looking for Melanie Hyde," Parker said.

"She lives in the back. In the cottage. You'll have to go around." The girl pointed to her right, signaling the men to walk to the driveway and circle the house. "Go up the stairs. She lives on the top floor." The girl, who was dressed for a tennis match, waited to see if there was anything else.

"Thanks," Parker said.

She closed the tall door as the men walked toward the driveway. They followed her instructions and found themselves at the door to Hyde's cottage, which took up the living space above a fourth and fifth car garage.

"Was that her sister back there?" Gray asked.

"I don't know. Nothing in the file mentioned a sibling."

Parker knocked on the door. Gray turned and leaned on the railing. He thought he'd be able to see more of the channel from the second floor, but all he really could see were the leaves from the tree-lined Channel Drive. They made him think of his dream.

The door swung open. He turned. The woman in the doorway was tall and lean. A little too lean, if Gray had to admit what he thought of her. She was shoeless but had on jeans, a blouse, and a light colored blazer.

"Well, I know you're cops, but I don't know why you're here."

"That obvious?" Gray replied before Parker could.

"To me, at least." She got right to business. "What can I do for you?"

"Melanie Hyde?" Parker asked.

"That's right."

"We're from Lakeland Police."

With that, she knew exactly why they were there.

"Shit."

Hyde bit her lip, which made Gray wonder if that was a nervous tick or if she was considering slamming the door in their faces.

"Come on in."

CHAPTER 10

Ten and two. Gray drove the interstate in the rain. A swirling wind whipped blankets of precipitation at the windshield. Ahead, he saw cars pulled to the side, waiting for the forceful rain to let up, hazard lights blinking. Others drove with their hazards on. Most of the cars still driving traveled between 40 and 50 MPH. Then there were the idiots who were still blasting through the blinding weather at 80. Not to mention the fools whose headlights were powered off. Gray could see fine at 45 MPH, so he maneuvered into the outside lane and just decided to call it home until the storm passed.

At first, the storm interrupted his train of thought about the case, but the concentration he needed for driving weakened like he hoped the rain soon would, and his thoughts returned to the day. *Melanie Hyde.* She'd invited them into her cottage and had told Gray and Parker that she backtracked her police report because one of her friends was attacked by the same man. She hadn't heeded the man's threat, so the attack on her friend was her fault. The years of drug-use that followed acted as her self-penance. However, in the last three years, she cleaned up and became the director of development at a women's shelter in Tampa, and that had slowly softened her emotions and thoughts about her rape. She felt like she was ready to talk about it, but she hadn't yet spoken up. Therefore, she had told them, they had showed up on her doorstep at the right time.

Hyde told them everything.

They walked away with a full account of the rape. Description of the man. Her friend's name. Everything she could recall. It dumped out of her like the rain was now dumping from the sky – in waves, with a blasting force, and cold. Gray worried about her emotionless retelling of the incident. She reminded him of Davis Islands, how they were built via nature and then expanded by the mud dredging of the bay. He thought of how her innate, natural existence had been dredged by the rape, and all that remained was a combination of the two. She still existed and even thrived in life, but the foundation was steeped in other people's decisions and actions.

All of that made Gray think about Morgan Beringer. Everything seemingly made him think about her. It was the oddest thing still, his tiny obsession with her. He remembered how she looked the night he'd met her. He recalled her wit and playfulness. Then her anger the last time they'd spoken. Those thoughts led him back to Parker and Vandenhill. His therapist used him. He used Parker. Hell, he was using the internal politics at the department too. By calling in the anonymous tip that got Cannon interested in the case, he'd manipulated everything and everyone. All of this was because of someone's manipulation. Finally, he thought of Vandenhill's patient. The woman whose story compelled Vandenhill to approach Gray. He'd not learned her name. Knew nothing about her, except her version of the story Vandenhill recorded. A story that matched Hyde's version. And Morgan's too. He wondered how the patient was. Then he thought again of Morgan. Nothing in particular this time. Just … her.

CHAPTER 11

The rain finally had stopped and so had Gray's thoughts about the case and the people surrounding it. It wasn't long before he had drifted off to sleep. Another night spent sleeping in his car. He woke with the sunrise and headed right into work. He took his go-bag from the trunk and then showered and dressed inside the locker room.

At his desk, he ate a candy bar from the vending machine and drank a cup of coffee brewed in the department's kitchen. Gray reviewed the paperwork Parker had finished from the day before. He didn't have anything to add about their interview with Hyde. Next, he searched Parker's desk for the results of searches in VICAP and the national sex offender registry. Parker was going to search for any cases with a social media link, and then try to narrow it down from there. Since there were no files or notes yet, Gray assumed the social media connection returned too many cases to narrow down.

"Are you kidding?"

Gray turned toward the voice. Parker stood behind him, frozen in the path from office door to his desk. He stared at Gray's coffee cup.

"It was your turn. *Again.*"

Gray sighed. Shoulders slumped. "Sorry."

Parker turned around and headed toward the office door.

"Wait," Gray said. "Where are you going?"

"To get my own coffee apparently."

"What about the search results?"

"No," Parker protested. "Not before coffee." He threw the door open and left the office in a huff.

Gray watched the door close before turning back to the file in his lap. The door opened again.

"Hey. Come out here."

Parker leaned inside the doorway. His face appeared more sunken than when he'd just left the room. Something else hadn't gone his way.

"What is it?"

"Just come on."

CHAPTER 12

"You assholes."

Maddy James led the two detectives on a walk around Lake Mirror, which rippled just south of the department headquarters building. They traveled down to and followed the Frances Langford Promenade circling the lake. Named after the radio and movie star, who grew up in Lakeland, the promenade was dedicated to the entertainer in 1946 for her work with the United Service Organization. Most of that history was not common knowledge around town. The lake was more recently known as the home of Blinky, the one-eyed alligator, and even more recently where the Hollis Gardens – a beautiful botanical display donated to the city by a Lakeland family – were located.

"Every time I get involved with you two, it ends up making my life more difficult."

"Every time?"

Gray pressed back at her without even knowing what she was talking about. Mainly because he didn't like the use of words like every, always, never, none, and all. They were too absolute. There was no way something happened *every time* or it *never* happened. *Sometimes*, sure, but not *every time*. Plus, the two didn't get along well. He thought her incessant flirting with Parker showed she was too young and inexperienced to be the chief crime scene investigator. She thought he was rude, self-centered, and jealous of her and Parker's friendship.

Parker stepped in before Maddy could react to Gray's question. "What are you talking about?"

"I'm talking about probably twenty different cases. Do you know what that's going to do to my department? And the politics? Holy shit. Boudreaux's going to blow his lid." Maddy stormed ahead of them, moving further down the sidewalk. Hand on her hips and shaking her head.

"You need to get your girlfriend under control, Jeff," Gray said.

"I've never seen her like this."

They picked up the pace, following her.

"And she's not my girlfriend. Quit saying shit like that."

They caught up to Maddy at a brewing company, crafting local beers onsite to be served to thirsty patrons in their restaurant and bar styled seating area. The restaurant area wasn't open for business this early in the morning, so there was no waitress offering them chilled, watermelon-infused water, which would have been refreshing after the nearly half mile walk in the sunshine and heavy humidity left behind by the rain the night before. At the outside table stationed on a patio overlooking the lake, the scenic promenade, and the gardens, Maddy had interlocked her fingers together in front of her mouth, rested her elbows on the table, and was nibbling at her fingernail without chomping it off or chipping the coloring.

"What's going on?" Parker asked.

She pulled her thumbnail away from her mouth and leaned against the back of her chair. Her posture slouched, weak, and tired looking. Her hands in her lap. She waited a minute, collecting her thoughts, before speaking. "This cold case you brought me. It's a mess."

"What'd you find?" Gray asked. He wanted to get to the point. What he saw on display in front of him was her emotional reaction to her findings. He wasn't one to deal with that.

She leaned forward and rested her elbows on the table again. She felt her blouse grab onto her sweaty back. "Four years ago. The department shake up. You remember that?"

They both did. It was discovered the then-chief of police was having an affair with two saleswomen of vendors who contracted with the department. Not only did that ruin the man's marriage, but it put the focus on those vendor contracts. The newspaper immediately began investigating. Those reporters smelled blood. They discovered that the contract bids accepted from those two vendors were competitive with the other bids, being only slightly higher in overall cost. However, these contracts included a larger payout to those saleswomen, contained an extremely high early termination penalty, and contained an automatic renewal of the contract two years before the contract was set to expire. One lawyer called them the most disgusting written contracts he'd ever seen, and he lambasted the city attorney for allowing the execution of them.

Not stopping there, the editor hypothesized in a true trickle-down scenario that if the chief of police was behaving in such a way, then the subordinates too were likely acting the same way. And that hypothesis proved correct. Though not with contracts and the department's budget.

The reporters uncovered a pattern of sexual misconduct, harassment, and intimidation within the department. They detailed every savory morsel they could uncover, like officers forcing themselves on civilian staff members – a couple even being traded like property; favors of all kinds being accepted in trade for ticket-fixing, avoiding arrest, and so on; and intimidation of other officers who were not taking part in these immoral and possibly illegal acts.

The newspapers flew off the shelves, spiking sales to record highs. Truth be told though, the reports painted the corruption department-wide. Yet in actuality the stories only focused on four officers, who were dumb enough to send each other emails about their escapades, essentially documenting what they'd done. Where the department went wrong was, most – if not all – of the staff members knew what was going on, and no one did anything to stop it. One officer was quoted in an article on condition of anonymity asking, "When two of the top-ranking officers are involved in these activities, who would we report the problems to?"

"That's when Boudreaux was promoted," Gray said.

The city commission considered dismantling the department and handing over the policing of the city to the county sheriff. Instead, they hired a third-party investigator to delve into the allegations and provide recommendations. The department didn't have a traditional Internal Affairs department, so the commissioners felt a neutral third-party would be best suited to handle the situation. The investigators recommended the firing of almost a dozen personnel, and they performed an extensive search for replacements for those high-ranking officers. They found that outside candidates were the best option in some of those positions. For the other positions, they offered suggestions for department restructuring and using current staff to fill those roles.

"And when I got my job," Maddy replied.

"I remember," Parker said.

One of those two top-ranking officers, Captain Roger Edgerton, managed the crime scene unit, which Maddy now supervised.

"And therein lies my problem," Maddy said, "and brings me back to you two being assholes."

"Tell us."

"I pulled the reports and samples of the cold case you brought me. Edgerton controlled the chain of evidence on that case. Now I know the victim recanted her complaint, but there was enough time that went by that the kit should've been tested prior to her recanting. But it never was. Florida at that point didn't have a backlog of rape kits to test. Not like New York City did. It just wasn't tested. Like, it was lost in time."

"We can test it now, right?" Gray asked.

"Of course," she said. "That's not a problem, and it's not *the* problem." She felt her make-up getting thick. She wrapped her curly hair in a bun as best as possible, hoping to get some air circulating across the back of her neck.

"What is *the* problem, Maddy?" Parker asked.

"I don't know why I did this. I really don't. Part of me wishes I hadn't. I checked other cases where he controlled the chain of evidence. There were a lot of them. He followed protocol on all of them. All except about twenty. Eighteen to be exact. All eighteen were rape cases."

"Son of a bitch," Gray said, connecting the dots.

"All of those kits went untested," Maddie said

Gray and Parker leaned on the table, propping themselves on their elbows.

Maddie sighed. "All the women recanted their stories."

Gray slammed his fist onto the metal table top. He thought immediately of Morgan Beringer and how she was raped by someone she probably knew or knew of because of her husbands' involvement with the police department.

"You have to test those kits," Parker demanded

"I know."

"We need that DNA. Without it, we don't have a case." Gray thought out loud. "Statute of limitations is four years in most of these cases.

And so far there are no reports of weapons having been used, so we can't file an aggravated rape against him, which doesn't have a statute."

"But, we have a year once the DNA is discovered, so, Maddy … " Parker was pleading with her. Almost desperately.

"I know, Jeff. I know."

"Start with the oldest case you have. Maybe he made a mistake back then while he was perfecting his assaults."

"We need to check for other more recent rape reports that were recanted," Parker said. "Maybe talk to those victims. See what they'll tell us."

They stood up from the table together to make the walk back to the department.

"Maddy, keep a lid on this for now," Gray said.

"It's going to be hard."

"Do it." Gray's tone stung. The order left no options for her.

"Again, you two are assholes for putting me in these situations. For how long, Gray?"

"Until it's time. I don't know." He barked at her, which sent her on ahead.

"We need to tell Cannon, Becker."

"Not yet."

Gray followed Parker. They were only a few steps behind Maddy. Gray kept his voice low, hoping Maddy wouldn't hear him.

"All that talk about the city commission and that third-party investigator reminded me of something. Cannon was next in line to be chief. The commission didn't recommend her. They skipped her and recommended Boudreaux. Whatever they didn't like about her wasn't enough to recommend her firing, but it was plenty for them to pass her over for the promotion. With all this connecting to back then, I don't want to tell her shit, Jeff. Let's see what we get first."

Maybe Gray was right. Parker worried about the position he was now in. "She wanted me to present the latest findings to the cold case unit committee. Today at four."

"Make something up." The words stuck in Gray's throat. Vandehill had told him the same thing when he protested this forced involvement in this. Here he was, doing and saying the same thing. To his best friend. He didn't like himself much right then.

Parker laughed, not appreciating Gray's simplistic approach. "Make something up. Yep, it's just that easy."

Gray pushed past not liking himself and stuck to his guns. "You can tell her the truth, if you want, but if she's connected to any of this somehow, then you know what'll happen."

"We're assholes, Becker. Just like Maddy said."

Still in earshot, Maddy said, "That's what I said. Everything with you two turns to shit." She quickened her steps, pushing ahead of them, ready to get to work and stop listening to them talk.

"Maddy," Gray called to her. He waited until she stopped and turned. "Good job."

She nodded and continued ahead of them.

"Is that high praise from you?" Parker asked.

"No. She just did a good job." Gray didn't want to get off topic. "Where can I get a picture of Edgerton?"

"Why?"

"There's an errand I want to run."

Parker froze, realizing how the pieces of this case came together. "Hey." He grabbed Gray by the arm, stopping his advancement too.

"What?" Gray looked at Parker's big hand wrapped around his bicep.

"Where are you going?"

"An errand." Gray pulled his arm from Parker's grip.

"No, Becker. Not this time. You're going to tell me where you're going with Edgerton's photo."

"No, I'm not." Gray stepped away from Parker and headed up the incline on Main Street nearing Massachusetts Avenue.

"Did you call in that anonymous tip?"

Gray stopped walking. He wondered why he didn't figure out in advance how he would reply if someone asked him that question.

"Gray," Parker called to him.

Gray turned around. "It doesn't matter. Come on." He shuddered at the stupidity of the response.

"Don't do that shit again." Parker commanded.

Gray wasn't going to admit the truth, but he didn't want to lie anymore either. "Can we just go back inside the building?"

Parker slowly walked toward Gray. The hurt of betrayal visible in Parker's eyes. Gray didn't often notice Parker's size, but he did right then. He didn't often notice his strength either, but Parker jammed his finger in Gray's chest, which made the man's power very clear. "Don't use me like that again."

Gray wanted desperately to grab his pectoral muscle, to soothe it from the bruise that was surely forming, but he didn't. Instead, he stood there stone-faced, hating himself for having manipulated his friend, wondering why he knew he should apologize but wasn't going to.

Parker huffed out a breath, like a bull, and brushed past Gray. He didn't look back, which pleased Gray because he could finally soothe his chest muscle. Plus, he didn't want to look Parker in the eyes again.

CHAPTER 13

The arrest of Roger Edgerton, a former captain in the Lakeland Police Department, was anti-climactic. He immediately protested his innocence and retained counsel. Instead of Gray hanging around the department, he let Parker stay and book Edgerton, who was going to lockup even if just until his arraignment. The district attorney would press for no bail, but Edgerton would probably be released with a high bond. He didn't see it playing out any differently than that, so he left.

The news hadn't picked up on the story yet, but they would soon. When they did, the reaction would be like a bright, white, hellfire explosion through the city. The newspaper would launch another attack at the department, searching for anything else even remotely inappropriate. The city commissioners might launch an investigation or go after Boudreaux, a response to the expected public outcry that a police officer could perpetrate rape and violence on the people he pledged to protect. Boudreaux would use his vast group of media friends to go on television and downplay the situation, to show he has control of his department and to reaffirm his faith in his staff. Boudreaux was a master at the media game.

Gray shrugged all of that off. It was all posturing. Newspaper and television need sales, and stories sell. Commissioners will look to be re-elected, and they need to appear as though they took action in light of this information. And the department would need to show they can be trusted. It was a game. A game of money and survival. All in all, this once again led back to the corruption that occurred years ago, so Gray figured, aside from some extra scrutiny, nothing would really come out of this.

His car stopped outside Morgan and Douglas Beringer's home. To Gray, after arresting Edgerton, there was only one other outcome that mattered in this case. *Morgan.* He walked to the front door, a file folder in hand. Gray wanted to talk to her alone, and this was the perfect time. Maybe the only time. Any minute the news of Edgerton's arrest would reach Douglas's office, which would set off a chain reaction of preparation for the media onslaught bound to occur. So, Gray figured, if Morgan was home, she'd be alone.

"Becker."

The front door almost acted as a shield between the two of them. She expected him to talk, but he didn't. The folder caught her attention, and she knew he was there on business again.

"Come in."

The island counter in the kitchen separated them. It was like these were their assigned positions – Morgan closest to the center of the house, with her arms crossed, and Gray closest to the front door, bearing news that would change her life again.

"What do you have there?"

Gray set the folder down on the counter.

"Last time I left here thinking I wouldn't see you again. I'm glad that wasn't the case."

Since his daughter died, the statement was the closest he had come to expressing to anyone how he felt about him or her. He hoped his nervousness wasn't obvious.

"And I thought the same thing about you and cop work, yet you and that folder are here in my kitchen."

"Right." Gray pushed the folder to her. "Open it."

"I think I'd rather not."

She wanted to just make him leave and take the folder with him. She didn't know why she didn't do that. She actually was excited to see him at the front door. She didn't know why, but she wasn't going to explore it either.

"I told Douglas what happened, like you suggested."

He didn't know what to say, so he didn't say anything. He just looked into her eyes. The pain he had seen before was still there. Maybe confusion. Maybe hope, too.

"Seemed to help, but I asked him to stay out of it." She crossed her arms.

Gray wanted to make her pain go away.

"He has, I think. Unless you're here to tell me otherwise."

"I'm not."

"Then what?"

"Open the folder."

She deliberated whether or not to do so. She studied his eyes, which he fought to keep steady. In them, he didn't want her to see his innermost thoughts of her. He must've been successful because she finally broke eye contact and touched the folder. She hesitated to open it, knowing the folder contained some truth that she probably wouldn't want to face. It was hard enough telling her husband that she'd been raped and handling the aftermath of betrayal Douglas felt for not having been told, for not having been allowed to be there for her, for believing for so long that he'd somehow lost her love.

She had thought that would be the end of it, the whole conversation, but that depended on the contents of that folder, didn't it? Tears rose in her eyes at the thought of it all, at the fear of having to possibly tell Douglas that she aborted a baby, unsure if it was his or a result of the rape. They'd been trying so hard for so long to get pregnant, she didn't know if she could bare it, if he could, if they could.

"I can't." She slid the folder back toward Gray, and she stepped away from the island. A guarded posture protected her.

"You told me that you used to face things head on. You have to now."

"Why?" She choked back her emotions.

"Because we caught him," Gray said.

She wasn't so sure, but she watched his face again to determine if he was telling the truth.

"And it's going to be all over the news, so you should prepare yourself."

Still she didn't say anything.

"I'm not here for cop work, Morgan. I'm here as a friend. Someone who cares. I think you need to be prepared for what you'll see on TV." He pushed the folder back to her.

She reached out to the folder again, filled with the confusion brought on by a cocktail of fear and relief at the news of the arrest. Her trembling fingers gained grip on the two flaps and she separated them, opening the folder, spreading it flat on the counter. The first thing she saw was an arrest warrant. Most of it didn't mean much to her. She saw charges associated with rape, kidnapping, and assault. Then she flipped the page and saw a mug shot, blown up to 8.5 by 11 size. The face seemed huge. The size threw off her perception for a moment, but then she froze and her breath caught. She recognized the man in the photo. It was him.

She slammed the folder closed, and her breathing sounded like she was hyperventilating. Gray hurried around the island and touched her arm. She jumped, startled. Gray figured she may have been lost in that horrific memory. When she got her bearings and saw Gray, she realized he wasn't the man who had raped her. She slipped into his arms and accepted the embrace he wanted to give and she so desperately needed. Her heart pounded as fast as any he'd ever felt.

"I can't believe it," she whispered into his ear.

Gray didn't respond. He lost himself in the embrace.

"How?" she asked, finally letting go of him. "Who is he?"

He promised himself he wouldn't lie to her again. He let her go. He led her to the living room and sat her on the couch. He sat in an accent chair next to her.

"He's a former police officer. He was able, through intimidation of victims and having an intimate knowledge of police procedure, to squash the rape complaints that were filed when victims didn't heed his warning. We found eighteen cases where he had direct contact with the evidence in the crimes he committed. We then found four additional cases reported where he didn't have contact with the evidence. In all those cases, except for one, there was no DNA recoverable. When we questioned the victims, though, they identified him as the man who raped them. He went through exhaustive pains to conceal his DNA, but he was so sure of himself that he didn't cover his face."

"Did the DNA match in the case where you recovered it?" Her voice was mousy-weak.

"It'll be part of the ongoing investigation to get samples from him, then we can connect him to that one case. So … not yet. The case is good though. Every one of the women has identified him, and we're looking into more connections. Possibly more victims. He's been arrested, but we aren't done."

"And the girl? The one you first told me about."

Nicole Abernathy. Gray nodded. "She came forward."

"She okay?"

"Getting there."

Morgan pondered the concept of "being okay" and wondered if she was.

"It was him," she said.

Gray nodded.

"He knew Douglas?"

"It's likely."

"Did he attack me because of that?"

"I don't know." He wanted to reassure her more. "That doesn't seem to be how he operated."

She nodded and then asked, "What now?"

"You face things head on again."

CHAPTER 14

The lightning show of another nighttime thunderstorm held Gray's interest as he drove Interstate Four toward Daytona Beach. The spindly strikes appeared briefly and looked like they were each stretching down to the Earth's surface. Gray wished they were angels' fingers reaching down from Heaven and plucking bad memories from the people who needed them plucked the worst. He offered up some names to the universe: Morgan Beringer, Nicole Abernathy, Melissa Hyde. Then he uttered his own name.

He merged onto Interstate 95 toward Jacksonville. The storm activity moved from his windshield to his passenger window, which freed his attention to focus elsewhere. He thought mainly of Morgan and her situation. He guessed the same was true for Hyde. And even for himself. *The past,* he considered. Each of them had buried their past deep inside them, almost entirely, and they pretended their pasts never occurred. For a long time that worked. But it did them no good. Not in the end. Gray had to face the loss of his daughter, and in hiding it, he broke his marriage and nearly destroyed his life with alcoholism. He still hadn't repaired his familial relationships, which shattered at that time as well. Morgan kept it hidden and almost ruined her relationship with her husband. Hyde tried to escape the pain by using drugs. Hadn't dated since the rape. She hadn't been able to keep a job. And was constantly in therapy. *How is all of that better than dealing with what happened to each of us,* he wondered.

No matter, right? Because the past came for each of them. Like an enemy who won't give up until it's defeated. *But how do you defeat it? Can you defeat it?*

Gray took the Ormond Beach exit on 95 and followed Granada all the way to A-1-A. He parked his Honda Accord in a resort parking lot and made his way around the property's fence to the beach. Staying careful of turtle nests in the dark, he made his way to the water's edge. His shoes filled with the grainy white sand as the lights from the street and resort faded away.

There has to be a way.

Gray had heard an interview on a morning radio show a few weeks ago. The morning zoo type deejays were interviewing – making fun of – a new age author. The whole time she was talking, they played cuckoo bird sounds in the background. She claimed if you stood at the mouth of a canyon, the brink of the ocean, or in the center of a wooded area and screamed out your pain, then the pain would be taken away in the wind. The echoes you'd hear were the wind carrying it away. So far that the scream would fade in the wind to a whisper before it disappeared.

Gray was finally at a point in his life where he was ready to try anything to let go of his daughter's death, to stop blaming himself, and to end the guilt of surviving beyond her.

He took a breath, opened his mouth, and screamed as loud as he could into the black sky. Spindles of lightning flashed in the sky above the ocean and its crashing waves. The echoes of his voice carried, softer and softer with each bounce back. A low rumble of thunder spread across the east coast of Florida, and then the echo whispers were gone.

ABOUT THE AUTHOR

Chris Wendel is best known as the author of the Becker Gray series. He is the solo *Medalist Winner* in the Suspense/Thriller category of the New Apple 2017 Summer eBook Awards for *Human After All*. He is also an author of books in the genres of business and poetry. He is a native of Lakeland, Florida, where the Det. Becker Gray novels are set. He still lives in Florida. Visit him at www.cwendel.com.

(An Excerpt)

THE
WALLS

A BECKER GRAY NOVEL BY

CHRIS
WENDEL

Holden Publishing, Inc.

PROLOGUE

"Can you hear me?"

Static crackled over the transmission.

"Shut up," the contract killer replied. He spoke into a device that fit snugly against his ear. A device he detested, but the man footing the bill insisted he wear so he too could hear the action, and since the killer was being paying handsomely, humoring the man seemed appropriate. *Just not putting up with any bullshit.*

"I need to know everything that happens." The voice came through a little muffled.

"Then you should be the one here," the killer said. "Shut up. If I tell you again, I'll throw this fucking thing away."

Indignant. "I don't like your tone."

Intolerant. "I don't care." The killer removed the device from his ear and jammed it into his sweatshirt's front pocket, careful not to disconnect the call.

The rear of the two-story, red brick colonial house opened onto an elaborate lanai, lit up by flood lights at each of the house's corners. The killer stepped onto the raised wooden deck and noticed the well-tended flowerbeds of yellow, purple, and red blossoms surrounding the structure. A huge outdoor decorative rug laid center on the deck, creating a community area around an outdoor seven-piece dining set. In the right corner of the deck, a fireplace built of red brick reached high into the air.

He took the steps down from the deck to a stone walkway leading to the house's back door. There was supposed to be a key hidden under the Louisiana State University gnome lawn decoration situated in the flowerbed closest to the French doors. His gloved hands leaned the gnome on its side, revealing a door key. *Good.* Despite gathering his own information on the target and planning the murder, the killer still had to rely on the man on the phone for assistance. That reliance made him nervous. *People who hire hitmen aren't exactly trustworthy folks.* He was ready to abort the whole contract, if even the slightest thing went wrong.

He'd been told once he had the key, entry would be smooth and quiet since there was no alarm system. *I'm about to find out.* The key fit neatly into the dead bolt securing the French doors. He turned the key, releasing the bolt's protective hold, then he slipped it in his sweatshirt pocket along with his earpiece.

He turned the knob, feeling the clink of the internal components. He took a breath, preparing his body to run in case of an alarm, then exhaled and pushed the door open. But, there was no sound. No alarm. His tension released. He stepped into the living room then closed and locked the back door behind him.

Scanning the house, he saw a digital clock – exactly three-thirty in the morning. The house was peaceful and still. Quiet – *for now.* An 80-inch flat screen TV sat perched on the mantle of a grand fire place. *Another fucking fireplace? In Florida?* The living room had three expansive, beige cloth couches surrounding a dark coffee table. *How mundane.* He pulled a snub-nosed .38

from his waistband. He wanted to kill the couple simply for the plain ordinariness of their home.

Climbing the stairs, he had a difficult time ignoring the family portraits along the wall. They reminded him of his own family. Except here in these photographs, there were no children. *Just the perfect-looking couple.* He took each step on the staircase slowly, focusing on stealth movement. Once at the top of the stairs, he surveyed the surroundings. Master bedroom immediately to the left. A spare bedroom to the right and down the hall just past a spare bathroom. A linen closet in the hallway across from the bathroom. Same as he'd memorized from the map provided to him by the man still making noise in the earpiece. *Shut up already.*

He stepped slowly to his left until he could peer into the master bedroom. The only light in the room came from the large window on the opposite side. A love seat took up space under the large window. A six-drawer dresser with a mounted mirror sat parallel to the king-size bed. Bathroom to the left.

Against the backdrop of that light, the killer could only see a silhouette of bodies. Couldn't tell detail from the door, but he could see there were two bodies in the bed. Lying still. All he could hear was rhythmic breathing, a little snoring coming from the man. *Good.*

The killer rounded the bed to the husband's side. His eyes settled upon the man. Details became clear. Athletic man. Mid-forties. Graying hair. Slept on his back. *That's the snoring.* The killer lifted the .38 and pointed it at the man's head. A surge of power built inside of him, making him stronger and his senses keener. *It's time.* He gave the man three last breaths. *One.* In and out. *Two.* In and out. *Three.* In and – *Bang! Bang! Bang!* Quick. Successive. Definitive.

The man's soul released. The body done. Blood and parts everywhere.

The man's wife sprang to life at the noise. *Fear. Shock. Adrenaline.* All at once. All overwhelming. She saw the scene. The man standing above her bed. Fight-or-flight kicked in instinctively. With a terrified scream, she made a run for it. Didn't even realize her husband's body shrapnel rested on her face, tangled in her hair, and clung to her long silky nightgown. Her heels hit the floor hard as she ran out the bedroom door toward the stairs.

I love a runner. The killer moved to catch up with her. As he started down the stairs, he could hear the voice through the headset in his pocket, screaming and laughing. Just as the wife made it to the last step on the staircase, the killer caught up to her. Gave her a small push. Adding to her momentum, the extra force of the nudge made her legs fall out from under her. She tumbled hard and rolled into the dark living room. Landed near the front door. Was slow to move after that. The killer came to a stop two steps from the ground floor. He hopped off the stairs, playfully. Again the feeling of power built inside him.

On the floor with her back to him, she moved to her hands and knees, sobbing audibly. She inched her way toward the front door, mumbling a plea to spare her.

"Turn around. I need to see you."

"Please, no," she whimpered. "Please let me go."

"Don't make me tell you again. I need to see your face."

The wife slowly, delicately turned her body toward him. Her hip hurt. Her ankle throbbed. None of that mattered to her though. There was something much more important that she worried about.

"Please don't hurt me. I'm pregnant." She kneeled in front of him, sobbing and rubbing her protruding stomach. Hugging it. Protecting it.

What? He hadn't noticed when he entered the bedroom or when she took to a run. If he had, he would've aborted the whole job, walked right out of the bedroom and down the stairs, out the French doors. He would've locked them and returned the key, like he'd never been there. But the man on the phone hadn't informed him of this important detail. And his own intelligence report, which had so much information in it, contained nothing about this. *How?*

The feeling of power ran low but was replaced by fury. He reached into his sweatshirt pocket and pulled out the earpiece.

The voice was still screaming and laughing, but the killer angrily yelled over him. "She's pregnant!" He yelled again, "She's pregnant. You didn't tell me she's pregnant!"

The voice continued laughing. "Who cares? Kill her anyway!"

"This wasn't part of the deal."

"Please," said the wife, seeing hope in the killer's hesitation. "I'm due in two weeks."

"Kill her." He wasn't laughing anymore.

"This wasn't part of the deal!"

Another whimpered plea. "I won't tell. I promise."

"Kill her!" The voice kept pushing.

"Please don't!"

"You're wasting time. You've already killed her husband. Someone heard the gunshot. You have to get out of there."

The killer needed time to decide what to do. Time to contemplate the options.

Static crackled again. "Do you want the rest of your money?" he yelled. "Kill her!"

I don't care about the money now.

Then the voice fell silent. The only sound in the room was the wife. Weeping. Praying. Pleading. She was an attractive woman, even without makeup. Even with red, puffy eyes. Even with tears merging with her husband's blood on her face. Yet his hesitation had nothing to do with her. None at all. She didn't matter.

It's the baby.

"Please don't kill my baby."

Anger was quick to enter him. Quick to leave, too. He felt it seeping out of his muscles, leaving him with a feeling of tiredness. He whispered to her, almost apologetically, "This wasn't part of the plan." His index finger nervously tapped against the trigger guard.

CHAPTER 1

Yellow crime scene tape lined the property surrounding the red brick colonial house, owned by the city of Lakeland's mayor, Douglas Beringer, and his wife, Morgan. Detective Becker Gray took in the scene as he walked from his 1993 Honda Accord toward the house. He had parked six houses away on account of the 23 varying vehicles parked closer to mayor's house – ambulances, police cars, fire department paramedic trucks, crime scene vans, news vans, and at least a dozens of other vehicles lined the residential street. The people who'd arrived in those vehicles buzzed around the area.

Chief Reginald Boudreaux held court in the center of all the chaos with a group of city and county officials gathered around him. Shock, grief, and confusion took turns on each on their faces. A gaggle of nearly 25 reporters and cameramen had been cordoned off to the side of the property and were under the watch of uniformed patrolmen.

This can't be real, Gray thought.

Noticing Gray slip under the taped boundary, Detective Jeffrey Parker flashed a subdued smile. Gray saw it immediately – something horrible hid behind the warmth of his friend's greeting. Parker left the front door of the house and walked down the narrow sidewalk toward Gray.

"How was vacation?" the 6' 6", 310-pound man asked.

"It was fine," Gray responded in a dismissive tone.

They shook hands. Parker noticed Gray avoided eye contact.

"You didn't go on vacation, did you?"

"I did. I haven't been to work in two weeks."

"No," Parker said. "I mean, you didn't go anywhere on vacation, did you?"

Gray didn't want anything to do with that conversation. He'd been forced by his therapist to take a vacation. He didn't want a vacation nor did he feel like he needed one, so he compromised. He took time off and told everyone, including his therapist, he was going to Aruba.

Gray, changing the subject, nearly whispered when he spoke, which drew Parker toward him. "What am I going to see in there?"

Parker shook his head, letting silence respond for him.

"It's really both of them?"

"It's ugly in there, Becker."

Morgan Beringer's blood-speckled face appeared etched permanently with worry and tension. Her body displayed three feet from the front door and covered with a plastic sheet. Only her shoulders, neck, and head still exposed. From under the edge of the sheet, Gray could see that blood had pooled around her body. The hollowness of shock overtook Gray. He looked away only to see the splattering of blood on the nearby beige cloth couch. Then he saw is on the walls, even on the stairs beyond her body.

The sight of Morgan Beringer, of her worried face destabilized him. His legs seemed rubbery. His arms weak. He disconnected from his body. Numbness set in. He didn't know if he was breathing, blinking, standing, falling. Nothing. He just wasn't there. *And this can't have happened.*

"Becker?" Parker noticed the change in Gray's posture.

They hadn't even made it through the front door yet.

"When's the last time you saw them?" Parker asked, gripping Gray's arm in support.

The pressure on his arm gave Gray awareness. "What?" he asked. He could tell the blood had drained from his face.

"How long since you saw her?"

"A while. I don't know right now."

Douglas Beringer was well-liked among the police department staff. He had served as a Lakeland police officer for 12 years before heading into the legal field and later into local politics. Beringer had hosted many gatherings at his home while campaigning, and he'd continued to do so even after he'd been elected mayor. Members of the police force were invited to every gathering he hosted. Gray had attended one of those gatherings – the Beringers' annual holiday party. Morgan had noticed him taking refuge from the evil of small talk. She had flitted through the attendees and sidled up to Gray. She talked to him, made him feel comfortable, even enchanted him. He thought of her smile then – soft and warm.

But, today her face had no smiles left.

"I was sitting down the street in my car," Gray said.

"I know. I saw you."

"I didn't want to come in here."

"I know." Parker also knew no one would stop Gray from going inside, so he didn't bother trying. "Let's go."

Gray turned back toward the body and watched Maddy James, the lead crime scene investigator, place a plastic bag over Morgan Beringer's left hand to preserve evidence. She wrapped a rubber band around the wrist, securing and sealing the bag. She worked gently. Respectfully. Easing Morgan's fair-skinned, slender arm back down onto the floor.

"Cover up her face." Gray's voice was quiet and stern.

Maddy hadn't noticed Gray enter. "Gray, you're back ... Great," she said sarcastically. Her thick, curly hair appeared like, if she were to move too quickly, it would break free of its elastic ponytail holder.

"Cover up her face," he repeated. He snapped at her, irritation at an all-time high. "She's right at the front door. People outside can see her."

"All right," Maddy replied. Exasperated. She grabbed the sheet, but before she pulled it completely over Morgan's face, Gray stopped her.

"Wait."

Maddy shot him a dirty look. "Are you kidding? Do it. Don't do it. Make up your mind."

One last look. "Yeah. Go ahead."

"Upstairs," Parker prodded Gray onward.

Parker pushed the master bedroom door open, revealing a cluster of technicians working the room. At the center of that effort lay Douglas Beringer. What was left of him. Douglas Beringer's face had been horribly disfigured by bullet blasts. Blood and matter were on the wall and spread across the bed except where Morgan had been sleeping. Shock again came calling.

"Why?" Gray whispered, not even realizing he verbalized the thought.

"I don't know." The booming voice of Chief Boudreaux was unmistakable. "This is the kind of shit-storm I hoped I'd never have to deal with again, and you two caught this call? The media's going to love this." He turned to Gray. "How was Aruba?"

Parker chimed in. "Right, how was Aruba, Becker?"

Numbness subsided, and sweat and chills simultaneously broke out across Gray's body. His breath quickened, and he could hear his heart beating in his ears.

"Initial thoughts?" Boudreaux asked when Gray didn't respond.

Parker gave the quick rundown. "Clean entry. Door must've been unlocked or the killer had a key. Very organized home. Nothing appears to be out of place. The safe is still locked. Valuables are still present. Doesn't appear to be a robbery."

For Gray, Parker's words were muffled. The room and his mind swirled like he had vertigo. Lightheadedness. Nausea. He loosened his tie and shirt collar, knowing he was going to lose control of his stomach.

The guest bathroom was right down the hall. The vomiting sensation held just long enough for Gray to make it to the toilet. His body dry-heaved, physically rejecting the Beringers' murders. It heaved a second and third time before relaxing from exhaustion. Out of breath and recovering, Gray sat on the tiled bathroom floor and leaned against the wall. Quiet blanketed Gray's mind just as Parker knocked on the bathroom door.

"You all right?"

Gray peeled himself off the floor. He heard blood rush through his ears. Black specs invaded his eyesight, but they disappeared quickly. He wiped the toilet rim with tissue and flushed.

"Just come out when you're ready," Parker said through the door.

The cold water refreshed Gray's face and hands. He rinsed his mouth. Leaning on the counter, Gray looked at himself in the mirror. Water drops, resembling tears, ran down his face. Over his left shoulder, he saw in the reflection three photographs on the wall behind him. All family photos. He wiped his face dry with the hand towel and turned to the photos. The one on Gray's left showed the Beringers in front of their Christmas tree. They were wearing matching ugly red and green sweaters. The one on the right celebrated a vacation in Washington, D.C. The Jefferson Memorial set in the background. The one in the middle showed the couple at the Polk Theatre. They were dressed in 1920s theme. Morgan looked lovely in her black flapper dress. Her posture seemed off though. Gray leaned closer to study the photo, wiping his eyes dry with the hand towel one more time. It was her hands, he decided. They weren't at her side or embracing her husband. They rested instead on her pregnant stomach. *Pregnant?*

Horror spread quickly across his mind. So fast, in fact, the bathroom walls converged on him, nearly crushing him and seemingly blasting him out the door as if he'd been launched from a canon. Gray thrust past Parker in the hallway and rushed into the spare bedroom where the horror intensified. The spare bedroom had been turned into a nursery. A half-built crib. Walls painted light blue. A dresser with a baby changing station across the top of it. A book shelf containing diapers, ointments, lotions, blankets and more baby products. A rocking chair in the corner. *No!*

Gray dashed down the stairs to where Maddy James was still working with the body of Morgan Beringer.

Out of breath, he demanded, "Pull it back."

"What?" Maddy replied.

"Pull it back."

"Are you kidding me?" A bundle of hair came loose from her ponytail as she protested.

"Becker." Parker reached the bottom of the stairs.

Gray couldn't control himself when he heard the tone of contrition in Parker's voice. He spun around and launched a finger in his partner's direction. "No! You should've told me."

Parker knew Gray was right. "Go ahead, Maddy."

As Maddy pulled the sheet back, it quickly became apparent there was more to this crime than Gray had initially known.

Morgan's long, cream-colored silk night gown was cut clear up to the collar, exposing her whole body to the people standing above her. Her pregnant, stretched-out stomach had been sliced, cut, and sawed open from hip to hip. Its contents had spilled out, collecting between her legs, flowing over her hips, and settling in a pool on the floor around her midsection.

Where's the baby?

www.ingramcontent.com/pod-product-compliance
Lightning Source LLC
Chambersburg PA
CBHW070505130626

46555CB00003B/1168